NATURE'S JUSTICE

NATURE'S JUSTICE

CA SOLE

Helifish Books

Published in 2019 by Helifish Books

ISBN: 978-1-9161108-3-0 (Paperback)
ISBN: 978-1-9161108-4-7 (eBook-ePub)
ISBN: 978-1-9161108-5-4 (eBook-mobi Kindle)

British Library Cataloguing in Publication Data
A CIP catalogue record for this book is available from the British Library

I am sincerely grateful to my wife and editors
who have provided invaluable input to make
this a better book.

Author's Note

The Scott Trilogy is about choice and consequence.

The first book, **Scott's Choice**, told how CJ Scott emerged as two separate individuals, Jonathan and Cuff, each following a different path through life.

In this book, **Nature's Justice**, Jonathan and his girlfriend, Gudrun, become embroiled in a highly dangerous situation in Southern Africa as they follow their instincts for adventure.

In the following sequel, **The Pilot**, Cuff embarks on a more stable career, but trouble seeks him out even though he tries to curb his natural tendency to confront risk head on.

Ideally, this series should be read in order: **Scott's Choice** followed by **Nature's Justice** and then **The Pilot**. You will understand why when you reach the end.

This book is written in British English. If you are used to reading American or another variation of English some of the spelling and punctuation may seem different, but it is not incorrect.

To move, to breath, to fly, to float, to gain all while you give, to roam the roads of lands remote, to travel is to live. ~ Hans Christian Andersen

PART ONE

Winter in Southern Africa

1

The man lay in agony on the far side of the mud hut, only three short strides away from most of the group. The wooden door was ill fitting and split where each shrunken plank had originally met the next. It hung on a single bent metal hinge with a loop of rope serving as the other, and was wired closed from the outside. Through the cracks came the only source of illumination, narrow beams of brilliance, rays of the harsh sun stabbing through the darkness to highlight, of all things, the woman who cradled his head, and, beyond him, the sack.

An uneven hum, the excited buzzing from a host of flies, formed a background of noise which was punctuated by the pitiful sound of the woman's quiet sobbing. The air inside the hut was still, the atmosphere stifling and heavy with the overpowering, acrid stench of a decade of cooking fires and a raft of disgusting and unfamiliar odours that sucked the oxygen from every breath the frightened tourists took.

Outside somewhere, a cow moaned at its thirst, and the shrill call of a woman carried from far away. A burst of childish laughter answered her. It seemed horribly out of place.

Sweat beaded on pale foreheads and trickled down sunburned necks. They were parched, but the dryness, the stickiness in every mouth, came as much from fear as lack of water.

2

The waterhole was not as isolated as its name suggested. It was only a short stretch of river which had not dried out. A buffalo would have its belly in the water in places, and the bottom had been churned to mud by the scores of hooves which, day after day, carried their owners into the shallows to drink.

At first, on that late afternoon, there was little to be seen. From their rented car, Jonathan and Gudrun watched a few impala and a small herd of zebra emerge from the bush and approach cautiously, desperate to slake their thirst, yet on constant lookout for predators.

When they had first met, Jonathan had been both fascinated and awed by Gudrun's eyes. Initially, as a stranger, he had stared into the icy blue of a deep and merciless crevasse and seen a distant, cold and unresponsive woman; until her easy smile and ready laughter shattered that impression. He soon came to recognise how, with no obvious change of expression, her eyes would soften by a fraction with humour or love or friendship, or harden with anger or determination.

Now, when she turned to him, those eyes were kind and soft and full of her enjoyment. 'This park is such a complete contrast to my little island. It's huge, a fifth the size of Iceland, yet is so empty. We have only about three people per square kilometre, which is fantastic for a western country, but here there's only the staff who are permanent. It must be a fraction of a person, a finger or toe in the same area; and so many animals! I'm having difficulty taking it all in. It's also hot,' she said, fanning herself with a map of the park. Her long hair was knotted into two braids she had pinned up over her head to let the air get to her neck. Even so, her shirt was damp under the arms.

'Thank God it's winter here, but it's still in the high twenties,' said Jonathan. 'We're just not used to it. It was only two months ago when we sat with Martin and Ginny at The Gargoyle, drinking beers beside the Thames, and told them what we were going to do. It was cool, it had rained, and our bums were wet from the bench – so different. Someone said it hasn't rained here for almost ten weeks.'

'They thought we were going to get married.' Her face softened with amusement at the memory.

'So did your parents. I found it quite awkward, because your mum kept looking at me, sizing me up, but we couldn't communicate at all. I was always relieved when you rescued me.'

'She thinks you're a nice man. So does my father. But she's worried you'll get me into trouble with all the risks you take.'

'I'm relieved your dad likes me, because he must be six foot six and tougher than one of your horses. I can see where you get your genes from. He's a good guy, though, and I could talk to him.'

'They're not world wise; they've never been abroad and don't often leave the farm. Look there!' Her long arm stretched out to her right, straight across Jonathan's nose, which he used to nudge it away.

The handful of impala seemed satisfied nothing was going to eat them, and took one cautious step after another down to the water. Encouraged, more of the antelope appeared from the cover of the bush until a sizeable group stood waiting.

'Look further left, that tiny wave.'

'What is it?'

Jonathan didn't answer.

'Oh God! Are we going to see something horrible?'

The first two impala put their forefeet into the water. A ripple of a presence below the surface tracked steadily in their direction. The antelope raised their heads, alert and suspicious. One took a nervous step back, turned and started up the bank. The second was about to follow, uncertain, torn between water and suspicion. It saw the danger and spun around. It took two steps and was almost clear of the pool when the crocodile launched itself out of the shallows, its whole body airborne in a massive leap.

Gudrun gasped. Jonathan almost turned to her at the sound, but was captivated by the scene. The reptile's powerful jaws clamped jagged, pointed teeth on to a hind leg. The creature landed hard, splashing mud high up the bank. The impala struggled to tear itself away.

Gudrun was rooting for it, thumping Jonathan's shoulder with her fists. 'Come on, rip yourself free! Never mind your leg, get free.'

Crocs' teeth are for biting and gripping, not cutting, and the impala's flesh would not part. The poor thing was surely to be dragged into the pool. It fought, though. Its head was pointing up the bank, chin out, neck stretched and yearning for the high ground; its eyes were wild and desperate, its spindly legs pushing hard into the bottom. The water was churned to a muddy slush that flew in all directions, obscuring the view. The crocodile rolled with incredible speed, dragging its victim over with it and flipping its head under the water. The impala was already drowning, but still it struggled in its lost cause.

Again the reptile rolled a complete revolution, giving a brief glimpse of its ivory belly as the action ripped flesh off bone. The massive head tilted up to the sky and the meat disappeared down its gullet, whole. Another bite and the carcass was dragged out of sight below the surface. A final short-lived ripple served as the silent conclusion of a deadly struggle.

Jonathan released his breath at last. 'Bloody hell! That puts life and death in the wild into perspective.'

Gudrun stared at him. 'Raw, utterly raw. I always thought man was the most vicious creature.'

'We are. That big lizard was just having supper in the only way he knows how.'

'Mister Scott, this car is tiny. I need to get out.'

'Don't be daft, Miss Einarsdóttir. Your trouble is that six foot two inches is too long for little cars.'

'I'm joking *Sæti*, but I do have to pee soon.'

'There's a lion lurking behind us.'

'Liar! More than a pee, I need a drink after that experience. Let's go back to the camp.'

3

High in the dust-laden sky of Mpumalanga, a vulture rode a column of hot, rising air in his unceasing search for food. The inescapable and merciless sun warmed his wings and reached below to scorch the already arid bushveld.

The summer rains ended in late March, with a couple of days in April that saw scant relief. By the end of May the pans were reduced to shallow, damp depressions, and the smaller rivers were waterless courses of sand. The rains were a forgotten phenomenon that might recur one day. Their absence had left the grass pale and tinder dry, and dehydrated trees shed leaves that crumbled to the touch.

The huge bird was the epitome of grace, gliding an orbit in the thermal with effortless subtle contortions of his massive wings. From this height he could survey all his realm, the two distinctly different parts divided by the most obvious feature, the straight line of the fence and the track which ran beside it; an alien, human thing, an unnatural and harsh ribbon scoring the boundary through the Lebombo Mountains and beyond.

The fence held no interest for the vulture save that it separated the land of plenty from one of nothing. He knew no boundaries, but in a sense it was his border too. For on its western side lay South Africa's Kruger National Park, a vast tract of land set aside for the preservation of the wild, a game reserve; for him, a storehouse of food. To the east lay Mozambique, ravaged in the past by civil war from which it had still not recovered. That and drought had brought extreme poverty, hunger and barbaric violence.

With eyes which could detect a mouse from a thousand feet, the great bird was able to see far into Mozambique, to a little collection of round, grass-roofed huts, the beaten earth, the pots, a great wooden pestle and mortar for grinding whatever maize the villagers could find, a few goats straining to reach crisp leaves on trees they had already shorn, and the listless, hungry people.

From the air, the village was like the hub of a battered wagon wheel, its crooked spokes the paths which carried starving cattle in a vain search for grazing. It was a dust bowl, the earth ground to a fine powder by countless hooves. Not a single blade of grass, nothing, was left to protect the surface and hold the fragile soil together. And so, if it ever rained again – for it seemed it never would – the precious layer would wash away as useless silt into the streams. The dreadful process of erosion, the creation of a desert, would resume its seasonal destruction.

It was not the village which held the vulture's interest, though, but four of its occupants who sat and crouched and lay in meagre shade on the western slopes of the Lebombo Mountains, from where they could survey a select area of the game reserve. Only the vulture saw them. To humans they were almost invisible, as their camouflage of tattered, sweat-stained clothing and dusty black skins blended with the background of the khaki earth and the mottled shadow of parched thorn trees.

The vulture kept an eye on these men, knowing what they

represented. His instincts led him to seek out death, for therein lay life for him. Kill or die; for the creature for whom every minute of every day is occupied with survival, and who, like the vulture, lacks or discards any recognisable powers of reason, any action that results in maintaining its own life is justified.

The vulture turned his attention further west. It might be some time before the poachers moved, and there had to be other, earlier chances of finding food. Although it held no interest for him whatsoever, he could not fail to see an open-top game-viewing vehicle leave the main road and turn down a track towards a small collection of rustic huts which faced the spot where the villagers lay concealed.

From where the four men hid, they could see deep into the reserve. Because of the drought the grass was thin, the grazing sparse. It meant animals were easy to spot, for they never strayed far from water.

A riverbed meandered from a break in the hills, marked by the dark green line of tall trees which clung to its banks and drew life from deep, subsurface moisture. The river no longer flowed; remnants of occasional pools which glinted in the afternoon sun were all that was left. A small herd of giraffe browsed not far from the banks, chewing slowly and rhythmically on leaves that only they could reach.

But giraffe were not what these men sought. There were easier animals to approach, and they had already chosen a different prey. When the time was right, it would not take long for them to track it down – and far less to kill it.

Normally, that would then be followed by the rush back over the border to safety with a load which would provide meat in the village for another few days.

But this occasion was different. This time they were after money, and that meant a prize to satisfy the greed of men in

Maputo who would, in turn, reap rich financial rewards from others in Bangkok, Beijing, Taipei, Hong Kong and Hanoi.

The poachers had spotted the rhino and her calf around noon, sleeping off the day's heat not far from the river. But it was too dangerous to leave their hide until much later. The camp under the opposite hill was always occupied, and the rangers were often on the move with their tourists. There was enough activity in the area for them to be wary of the daylight.

They argued. The more experienced said the moon was almost full, it was bright enough for them to track and shoot the animal and make their escape before dawn; a safe but more difficult option. The young and eager insisted there was no moon until the early hours of the morning, which meant they had a long wait ahead of them. They should leave their hiding place in the late afternoon, giving themselves enough time to kill the rhino at last light and escape over the border under the cover of darkness. This was the best option because pursuit was the most difficult. No, the older men retorted, that was a good plan but with any delay there would be no light by the time they caught up with the rhino. The shooters could miss, and to track a wounded animal before the moon rose would not be easy and would take much time.

4

Jonathan regarded the other tourists. There was Annette and Armand, a French couple; Claire and Kathy, cabin crew taking a few days off; Hudson Khunou, a black businessman from Johannesburg; and Mickey Rider, the owner of a haulage company in England. As he shook it, Jonathan felt the calluses on Mickey's large and heavy hand and sensed the overly-strong grip was there to demonstrate who was the dominant male.

They had gathered to spend two nights and three days in the wild being guided by a ranger in search of unspoilt nature, Africa as it was before man tried his best to wreck it. Eagerly, they anticipated their first exposure to lion and elephant, to rhino and a whole host of different animals and birds, all on equal terms because they would be on foot. It would be such a prize experience that an air of almost childish excitement gripped them. And, as most strangers will when put together in an alien environment, each sought friendship and solidarity with the others. Which was why the conflict struck such a sour note.

It began when the ranger, who introduced himself as

André, told them in his strong Afrikaans accent to jump into the open four-wheel drive which would take them to the bush camp. Mickey Rider was the first to move towards the front seat.

Jonathan had been looking the other way at the time and had not intended to obstruct Rider. He took the single pace necessary for his long legs to reach the door and opened it with an elegant flourish, thereby blocking Mickey's advance. Looking down his aquiline nose, he said pleasantly, 'Ladies, who would like to sit in front?'

He turned to find Mickey glaring at him; the man's fists were clenched and his lips were tight. Rider could hardly force his way in, so had been compelled to retreat and swallow his ill-mannered intention.

Gudrun said, 'I want to sit next to Jonathan. One of you two girls ride in front.'

Kathy, the shorter one, stepped forward. 'Thanks.'

Rider was the first to climb into the back to the next prime position, on the outside behind the driver. Eager to be on their way, the others boarded, followed by Gudrun. Rider gave her a cocky grin and patted the seat beside him. 'You sit here. You can always stretch across me if you want to see something special.'

Gritting his teeth, Jonathan sat next to Gudrun and placed a possessive hand on her knee.

She whispered in his ear. 'Let go of my leg, you're hurting me.'

'Sorry, I didn't realise.'

'Relax, silly. He's only trying it on.'

Jonathan simmered in silence; he foresaw an ongoing battle of wills. In front of him, Kathy was leaning across the car and listening to the ranger. At one point she touched André's arm, letting her fingers rest there a moment too long. André, appreciating the attention, was beaming at her.

What sort of social life did a bachelor in André's position lead here in the bush? Were there eligible women on the staff? How often could the ranger get out to meet girls? His was a different world.

Gudrun was watching as well, until Mickey leaned closer to her and whispered, but not so quietly that Jonathan couldn't hear, 'I get the picture, but if you need a change of scenery …? Know what I mean?'

'No,' was her curt answer.

Jonathan's temper flared. 'You should save remarks like that for the kind of women you're used to.'

Mickey's grin was wide, but his look was challenging. 'Keep your hair on. Just being friendly.'

Gudrun laid a restraining hand on Jonathan's shoulder and said, 'He's an alpha male, he wants to show who's boss, and you're his natural target. He's getting at you through me. I've seen lots of these guys, so I know. Don't antagonise him, please.'

As the car bumped along a dirt track, Jonathan wiped the sweat off his neck with a large red handkerchief. *How are the next few days going to develop?* It had promised to be an incredible experience, and he and Gudrun had been looking forward to it. But now, the presence of a man like Rider had the potential to ruin this time in the wild.

He looked up and admired the grace of the huge birds which wheeled and soared on the thermal of warm air thousands of feet above them. *Do vultures have their social problems as well, or are they solely concerned with food?*

The bush camp was situated at the base of a low hill. It comprised a pretty collection of thatched A-frame huts in no particular order, each one located to the best advantage beneath a large, spreading acacia. Almost hidden in the background was a more conventional shelter, which was a kitchen.

They climbed down from the vehicle. Rider appeared to be the only smoker; he lit up as soon as his feet were on the ground. The women made appreciative noises as they absorbed the rustic charm of the place. A clanking of pots and the smell of onions stirred hunger, although it was still a long time to supper. The ground had been stamped bare and hard around the huts and within a central, communal area, which held a few camp chairs and a table. Here the visitors would gather round an open log fire in the evenings, slaking their thirst, swapping stories and listening to the ranger telling them about the bush.

As André delved into the car and handed out their packs, two African game guards presented themselves, smart in green uniforms with brown boots and Parks Board epaulettes. The men stood still, a serious, impassive expression on each face, as if they were waiting for a cue to relax.

'Ah.' André indicated each in turn. 'This is Sipho. He'll come with us when we walk, and here is Petros. He'll stay and guard the camp. They're both excellent trackers. You can trust them with your life. But that won't happen, eh Sipho?' He grinned at the ranger, whose face softened with a gleam of white teeth.

Jonathan was the first to step forward to introduce himself. He had met black people before, of course, but they had been West Indians or British citizens, never from the African bush. But as he took each leathery hand with its surprisingly soft grip, he was reminded of the simple dignity displayed by rustic folk everywhere. *These two may not have had much formal education, but there's no doubting their intelligence, and they must be experts in their environment, which we tourists are not.*

Annette hovered on the periphery of the group. From one position to another, her camera clicked while the introductions were made. She was accomplished, going about her task almost unnoticed, the camera manipulated with such skill it appeared to be a natural extension of her hand. She was a plain-featured, but not unattractive, woman in her late thirties with a firm, slim figure and black hair which she kept in a bob. She and Armand were a pair, inseparable. They were even dressed for the bush in matching outfits of light brown slacks and shirts with identical floppy hats. It was easy for Jonathan to think of them as a single unit. *I hope people regard Gudrun and I like that.*

André, always interested in his clients and the lives they led – so distant from his own – asked, 'You seem to know what you doing with that camera. You professional?'

Annette cocked her head at an angle, her dark eyes widened, and she gave a slight smile. The movement was innocent and sensuous. '*Oui*, yes, semi-pro. Armand is a tour guide, a special one.' And she gave him a fond glance, stretching a hand out to him, even though it could not reach. 'We travel everywhere in search of good places for tourists. We find one, like this. It is most beautiful, exciting and we make the reconnaissance. I take all the pictures, and we return to France to put a tour together. Then Armand returns with his tourists and shows them the best of what we have seen.'

Jonathan and Gudrun glanced at each other. The French couple were already doing what they themselves were planning; it was how they wanted to live their lives, except Gudrun had no intention of being left behind on the trips.

Armand added, 'We go everywhere, the Amazon, Cambodia, America, but this is the first time in South Africa. Always we look for the unusual, the exciting. I don't take old ladies.' His mouth twitched in a brief smile. He was a small, thin man of about forty with hollow cheeks and swarthy looks. To Jonathan he seemed a serious person, one brimming with common sense, someone to turn to for a solution, any solution. But he would have to be asked for the answer, he was not one to volunteer his input nor to push himself forward as long as more voluble people were about.

Changing the subject, André said, 'It's not so hot now, if you like we can go for a short walk before sunset.'

There was an eager murmur from everyone. This was what they had come to do.

'Okay, we start in half an hour. Before that, sort yourselves a hut. There no need for the single people to share, unless you scared of the dark,' he said with a laugh.

'That's easy.' Without taking the cigarette from his lips, Mickey Rider seized Armand's arm and pointed. The smoke puffed from his mouth as if emphasising his words. 'You two go in that one there. You girls in the next, I'll take the one next door. Then Hudson.' He flashed a cold, contemptuous look at Jonathan. 'You two can take the one at the far end.'

Jonathan's expression betrayed nothing. With a level gaze at Mickey, he raised one brow, dropped it and said, 'I think that's a decision for everyone to take. Are you happy with that, Hudson, or would you prefer to be on the end?'

'Thank you. Yes, I like the end,' Hudson said, causing Mickey's jaw muscles to bulge.

Jonathan ignored him and, picking up both his and Gudrun's packs, strolled off to their hut. Like the others it had two beds, a narrow stoep and a washbasin on a stand. Each bedside table bore a kerosene lamp, a box of matches and a dish with a mosquito coil. A musty smell of thatch gave it a homely atmosphere. A window in the back wall was formed of mosquito netting. The wooden floor was raised well off the ground and creaked with every step.

Gudrun gathered her towel and wash bag and descended the creaky steps. To get to the ladies' ablutions she had to pass behind Claire and Kathy's hut. As she reached it, their voices were clear through the rear window.

'I think Gudrun's quite nice. Pity about her boyfriend; he's a bit stuck-up, isn't he?' That was Kathy's voice.

'No, not really. I think they're a nice couple.'

Gudrun stopped. She was not a nosey person, but when someone was discussing her, she, like anyone else, had to listen in.

She had a great reliance on first impressions and had known Claire would be a natural friend. She imagined her now, in the hut, heard but unseen: a round, pretty face, dimples in her cheeks, dark blue eyes and a dark pixie haircut. Intelligent undoubtedly, refined certainly, and one of those enviable women who manages to look elegant under any circumstances.

'Huh.' Kathy again. 'Thanks for dragging me on this lark. It's lovely isn't it? I've got a good feeling about it.'

'I told you you would, but if those two men don't put their hackles down it's going to spoil things a bit. Rider is obnoxious, don't you think?'

'He's only reacting to that snob. I think he's rather dishy, myself.'

'You would. It's one of the disadvantages of having the hots for the opposite sex; you can't always choose the best men.'

Why was Claire having a go at her friend?

Kathy's voice was loud and sharp this time. 'Well it's better than being frigid!'

'I'm not frigid, and you bloody well know it. I'm just better adjusted than you and choosy about my men.'

'Bollocks!' Kathy sniffed and cried, 'It's bloody easy for you to be "well adjusted", coming from your nice little home in nice little Cuckfield in nice little Sussex. You had a good family life. I didn't. I was born in my dad's bloody pub. My folks were so bloody busy I'm surprised Mum had the time to give birth, and I've hardly seen her since. The only love I've ever had was from blokes.'

'Yes, I know, and there wasn't a virgin left in your brother's platoon by the time you'd finished with them, and now you're working your way through the airline.'

There was a pause. Gudrun was about to move on, but the sadness in Claire's voice piqued her interest. 'I'm sorry. You've told me before.' A creak of movement across the floor created an image of the two now sitting together.

Claire's tone was comforting. 'Don't you see? Those men never gave you love. You can't find love that way.'

There was a long pause. Then Claire said, 'I'm sorry, I'm only trying to protect you from yourself.'

Another loud sniff. 'I know. You always do and I'm grateful – I am. You're the only one who cares about me. You make me feel secure, but you can't give me what a man can.'

'If it's any consolation, I need you too. I need your crazy ideas to show me the seamier side of life – which I quite enjoy.' A laugh. 'Look, if you must, why don't you try your luck with André? He's a decent chap, and he's better looking than Mickey. After all, I promised you a sexy game ranger to get you to come here.'

Kathy giggled. 'You promised me a herd of sexy game rangers, but you've only found one.'

'Sorry. I'll try harder next time.'

A hint of sadness coloured Kathy's next remark. 'You're right, but there's no future in André. You never know, I might find something with Mickey. I've never had a steady bloke, and thirty's around the corner.'

Gudrun moved on, feeling a little ashamed of herself.

5

It was late to start a walk, but André assembled the group and surveyed them before leading them in single file down towards the riverbed. With the exception of Mickey Rider, they had followed the advice to dress in neutral colours – slacks or shorts and shirts in various shades of brown and khaki. Mickey, on the other hand, wore a dark green camouflage-pattern shirt, and shorts of a dirty yellow. The trouble was that the shorts were not going to blend into the bush, and the shirt was perfect for hiding in some forest far from the dry, brown bushveld.

Being in the middle of a group was not Jonathan's preference, but since he could neither be at the front nor the back, there was no point in arguing. Mickey's frustration at not being able to lead was plain, however.

Why was this man in such a rage about life?

He took a deep breath as Mickey dictated in which order everyone should walk. He, needless to say, would be at the front of the tourists. He put Kathy behind him, no doubt to watch his muscular legs in action. Claire next, then Annette, Armand and Hudson followed by Gudrun and Jonathan.

Sipho, the ranger, was to take his allotted position guarding the rear. Both André and Sipho were armed.

Jonathan raised an amused eyebrow at Gudrun as Claire, resenting Mickey's dominance, ushered the French couple ahead of her to make a point. And Hudson asked Jonathan and Gudrun to go ahead of him, saying he wanted to chat to Sipho in his own language. This adoption of their own order contrary to his instructions caused a visible rise in Mickey's temper, and it took a while for him to settle down.

Although the heat of the day had subsided to the mid twenties, beads of sweat sprang from European pores and trickled down flushed cheeks as soon as everyone moved. André set an easy pace along a well-trodden game trail: a dusty, meandering path which carved its way between patches of sparse, desiccated grass. Grey-barked knobthorn with vicious, silvery spikes formed a formidable barrier in places, punctuated by the occasional darker, and taller, marula and acacia tree. Several of these were sad corpses, having been pushed over by elephants keen to get at their succulent roots, eat the bark and feast on the delicious fruit of the marula.

After twenty minutes, they reached the river and stopped on a high bank to rest and cool down. Sipho left them to scout for tracks. Knowing they were out for a short time, everyone had left their backpacks behind – only Jonathan and Armand had brought their water bottles. Armand passed his canteen to Annette, and Jonathan handed his to Gudrun, took a sip when she had finished and stretched to his limit to give it to Hudson.

Sipho appeared amongst them again, no one having seen him approach. He murmured something to André who stood and gestured for them all to gather round him.

'Sipho has found a black rhino and her calf,' he whispered. 'We'll follow him. He says they still sleeping, but soon they eat because it's getting cool now.'

'You could have fooled me.' Mickey took out a cigarette. He was red in the face and sweating profusely.

André stopped him. 'Not here, only in the camp, sorry. The animals will smell it, and the risk of fire is high.'

Mickey rammed the cigarette back into the pack and swore under his breath.

'Now listen,' André said in a low voice. 'They don't see good; if you stand still she won't spot you at twenty metres. But they hear well and their smell is also good, so we'll come at them from downwind. Always keep your eye on Sipho or me, and please keep quiet.' He wagged a finger at Annette. 'Ask me before you take your pictures, okay? The camera makes a noise.'

Jonathan glanced at Gudrun who made a face with a nervous grin, her bottom lip pinched between her teeth.

'Troops being briefed before battle,' he said.

As they approached with exaggerated care, they saw the mother was sleeping, her calf snuggled against her flank. Two enormous, grey, grotesque pigs with only their ears active, swivelling about like radar antennae as they maintained a vigil while their bodies recuperated.

André stopped the group about forty metres from the great beasts. The women were captivated by the calf. It was easy to imagine the 'oohs' and 'aahs' which would have gushed unrestricted had they been safe in the car. But all of them were awed by the situation: on foot, only paces from two tons of dangerous, prehistoric monster. Jonathan glanced at the others. Each of them had the same feeling he did: an overwhelming pleasure in being so close to the wild things.

Although the rhino slept, their sentries remained on guard. The resident oxpeckers stopped gorging on ticks from the thick hide and raised the alarm with a frantic chirping. The mountain lurched to its feet with surprising agility, instantly alert. In miniature, her calf sheltered close to the curve of her belly. She stood motionless, radiating suspicion. Her ears twisted to catch the slightest sound, and her nostrils flared, searching the wind for danger. She found nothing. The fuzzy images ahead were indistinguishable even though she was staring straight at the humans. But she knew something was there and wheeled, snorting and leading her baby away at a rapid, springy trot, its tail looped over its rump in tiny imitation of its mother. After a few metres, in a cloud of dust, she wheeled again to face the threat.

Annette was taking pictures, Armand close at hand. At each click of the shutter the rhino's ears twitched until she spun about and trotted away, her great bulk vanishing into the bush, her little calf close behind.

Jonathan put a hand on Gudrun's shoulder as she murmured, 'Ooh wow. They're so ugly, but they're also beautiful, not so? I would not believe I could fall in love with a rhino, but I have. They run around as if they're on springs, and yet they look so clumsy. That baby with its stub of a horn … André, please, can we come and see them again tomorrow? I'm sure the others would like it too.'

The ranger grinned up at her. '*Ja*, of course. They'll be easy to find.'

Jonathan looked for the others' reaction and was surprised at the soft expression on Mickey's face. Seen like that, no one could imagine the man harboured so much pent-up aggression ready to spew at the nearest suitable target. Lost in the past, the man said, 'When I was a kid, my dad would lay into me as if I was to blame for everything. We had a little farm; I'd run and hide with the cows. They was the only friends I ever had, them and Granddad. I had names for them all. I used to hug them and cry for hours until he'd got over it, or Granddad came to rescue me. I don't know why, but that dumb thing over there with her calf, she reminded me.

She's a mother, and a better mum than mine ever was. Look at her. Poor bloody thing, blind as a bat and probably scared as hell for her baby …'

It was no excuse in Jonathan's opinion, but was Mickey's father the origin of his perpetual anger?

6

André tossed another log onto the blaze. Sparks exploded, and a green stick hissed its protest. A warm glow reflected off the tree trunks and overhead branches, pushing back the darkness and creating the illusion of being enclosed within the security of an orange globe. Even the constant stridulation of cicadas was somehow remote. The night had turned chilly and everyone had put on a jacket or light jersey.

Having heard the two girls' discussion, Gudrun was watching Kathy's behaviour with interest. What was she going to do about the available men?

Kathy was more striking than pretty. She was short and stocky, the sort of cuddly figure which suited a young woman but would spread with children and advancing age. Her hair was fair and cut raggedly, with strands of varying length, giving her a wild appearance. Hers was an active face, with a narrow gap in her front teeth, dimples in her cheeks and a naughty expression. Gudrun smiled to herself, partly in admiration: sexy and flirtatious, this girl seemed to be perpetually on the point of doing something exciting or scandalous.

It was pretty obvious Kathy fancied André. Her flirting was overt, with her coquettish eyes and little fingers which reached out to touch his arm a bit too often. Gudrun had to agree with her: André was masterful and attractive. He was a well-built man of about thirty-five – he could have been younger, as a lifetime of exposure to the dust and dryness of the bush and an unforgiving sun had left its mark. His fair and unruly hair was bleached to an even paler shade, in contrast to his deep tan. And those intense blue eyes! It was easy to put herself in Kathy's shoes and imagine a night of lovemaking under a brilliant African moon.

'André, please tell us about yourself,' Kathy said. 'We want to know everything about the man who will keep us safe for the next few days.'

'*Ag*, no. You don't want to hear about me. You people have more interesting lives.'

'*S'il vous plaît*. André, really we are interested. You lead a life that is so different to anyone here.'

'*Ag*, all right, if you want.' He paused for quite a long time. 'I was born in the bush, and I've lived all my life in the bush. I know people from outside think all Africans are black. That not so. My folks and their folks before them and before that, they knew only South Africa. They did not know any other land – neither do I, and I don't want to. People can keep the big cities: Jo'burg, Cape Town, Durban … they not Africa. They the same as London, New York – I guess – just cities. The bushveld is Africa where its heart beat strong. I tell you, without the animals, the trees, the plants, the insects, birds and reptiles, Africa would be the same as anywhere else: a place for humans to destroy. So, I'm committed to nature. As a manager, I do my best to protect it from all the things that will destroy it.'

'What sort of things?'

'All sorts: fire, drought, over-population of elephants

inside the park boundary. Those are part of life, natural things. But I get sick to my gut about poachers.' He paused, then thumped his own stomach with a fist. 'I seen it so many times. I get so bloody angry I …'

Gudrun regarded him with interest. André's passion almost let him express something politically incorrect, something which might alienate a sensitive client.

He swallowed and lowered his intensity. 'When they come through the border fence and take a *bok*, an impala or a kudu so they can feed their family … I can understand, I can turn a blind eye; but when they come and kill an elephant for its tusks or a rhino for its horn, then it gets me. That's for money, not for life, and I won't forgive it.'

It seemed André's words had subdued Kathy. She studied him respectfully for a while after he stopped talking. But she was keeping her options open, by the look of it. With one hand lingering back in André's direction, she turned in her seat to smile at Mickey Rider.

Gudrun did not agree with Kathy on that man. He was not attractive. He had a powerful, tank-like build and took every opportunity to display his strength: a gym fanatic. He was fair with tight curly hair and a skin of the type which, instead of tanning, turns a painful pink. Much of the time his eyes were narrowed, and his jaw muscles worked furiously. He seldom stopped flexing his fingers and clenching his fists. *What is his constant anger about? Is it this simmering power which turns Kathy on?*

Whatever it was, the girl melted when Mickey looked at her.

I doubt if André is used to being manipulated like this.

Jonathan listened without comment as the conversation turned to discussing their occupations, to put meat on the bones of their knowledge of one another. Armand and

Annette had been whispering to each other and trying to look at Gudrun without being noticed. After a while, Armand could not contain himself. 'Do you play tennis?'

Jonathan smiled. He had made the same mistake when he first met her, so he knew Gudrun was well prepared.

She laughed. 'Yes.'

'Er … well? Do you play well?'

'They say I do.'

'You are amongst friends here, and there is no contact with the outside for unwanted publicity. Are … are you not truly Maria?'

Jonathan had his hand over his mouth, trying to hide his amusement. Gudrun was struggling not to laugh, to avoid appearing rude. 'I play doubles with Maria, and it is difficult for the opponents to know who is who.'

Armand and Annette, avid tennis fans, gave a collective gasp. 'What is she like?'

Claire and Kathy were listening with interest, but neither Hudson nor Mickey nor André knew what – or who – they were talking about.

Gudrun held up her hands. 'Please, I'm teasing you. I'm sorry, but I get this question in many forms all the time, and the best way for me to deal with it is to make a joke. I am not Maria, and I do not play tennis. Sorry. She does look like me, but I am one centimetre taller.'

Armand laughed at their slight embarrassment and, feeling a little foolish, turned to Jonathan. 'Is this your first time 'ere? I think it will be a fantastic 'oliday for you.'

'Honeymoon, perhaps?' said Annette with a mischievous expression.

Jonathan and Gudrun both laughed. 'No,' he said as he pulled his sleeves up his forearms, 'we're not married, and this is more a reconnaissance than a holiday, because we hope to do the same as you: conduct exciting expeditions for adventurous customers. This is our second exploration, the first was in Bolivia and Peru, where we met.'

'South America, eh? *Très* romantic,' Annette teased with her head cocked to one side. She raised her eyebrows and gave a wicked little grin, the tip of her tongue peeking out below her teeth. To tease and encourage lovers was fun and always boosted the relationships.

'Well it wasn't so romantic at the time, because Gudrun was arrested for murder.'

'*Mon Dieu!* That is not a good beginning for love.'

'Fortunately it was misidentification, but she had me worried for a while. I thought she might kill me in my bed.'

'I still might.'

Armand said, 'If we can assist with your project, perhaps share some experience, dos and don'ts, we will be glad to 'elp.'

'That's kind of you, and we're sure to take you up on it.'

Jonathan was watching the interplay between Kathy, André and Mickey with interest. There was something ugly about her manipulation of the two. Mickey appeared to be the one who turned her on, so why was she dangling André on a string? He watched her lean towards her target.

'What about you, Mickey? You're successful, what do you do?'

Rider was an unlikely character to be touring a game park in Africa. Jonathan was repulsed by Mickey's dress sense. The camouflaged shirt, he decided, was pickle on the curry of his turmeric shorts; it was awful. He should never have left the slums of whatever dreadful city had spawned him. Nevertheless, his reply would be interesting.

'I'm in trucking.' Mickey lightened up with the attention now centred on himself. 'I started with nothing, not even a driver's licence, but now I've got a bit more than a bob or two. But I've had to fight my way to the top. Result? My outfit's my own, and it's the best.'

Kathy, fawning over him, said, 'You must have worked hard to get where you are.'

'Yeah. It takes guts, a bit of savvy and a lot of bloody hard graft.' With an underhand look at Jonathan, he said, 'Some of us have to work for our boodle.'

Kathy picked up on his cue. 'And you, Jonathan?' she asked. 'You're obviously not working. I mean, you must have some sort of income to do all this travelling.' Her words were innocent enough, but they came from her while she was still leaning close to Mickey. It gave the impression she was asking on his behalf, and the query was therefore a loaded one.

Jonathan was surprised by the personal nature of her question. He would have told them how they were financing their current lifestyle, adding that it could not go on for much longer without earning something. But an irrepressible urge to present a contrary picture to Rider came over him. It would confirm the man's incorrect suspicions, and was dangerous because it might make the atmosphere even more unpleasant. He was not a man who avoided problems, however, and couldn't resist.

'In truth, little.' He kept his voice casual. 'I inherited a position on the board of a company in the City, but that's a chore which I avoid whenever possible. I also inherited the family estate, which is both agricultural and a stud farm. That's my primary concern, but I employ some jolly good chaps, and I have to admit it requires little direct participation from me.'

Rider nodded as if his suspicions had been confirmed. 'What do you do? Day to day, it can't be nothing at all.'

Gudrun was glaring at him. *She knows I'm going to add something well over the top, and she's not happy.* But he had chosen a course and would not change now. He decided to give the man something to chew on. 'Well, let's see, I have to make time for two weeks' skiing at Klosters in the winter, and I often spend a while in the Caribbean as well. In between, I play a great deal of polo and, believe it or not, the estate does require my small contribution. It is a business, after all.'

A pause followed while the group dwelt on this idyllic lifestyle.

Jonathan was concerned only with Rider. In doing so he'd created a gulf between himself and the others, who had become less receptive. It was too late to back out now, though, he could put them straight later. 'Of course, there are other commitments, like the grouse season; and my stockbroker keeps pestering me. But, in your terms Mickey, I am indeed most fortunate. However,' and Jonathan looked over the flames at the other man, 'what little I do *is* honest.'

'What the hell does that mean?' Mickey shouted and leapt to his feet, his cigarette dropping to the ground unheeded.

Even the crickets fell silent.

'Hey, guys …' André sounded ineffectual. It was most unlikely he'd ever had to deal with hostile guests before. Everyone else receded, their attention riveted on the antagonists, their faces expressing a nervous mixture of awe and disgust.

'I asked you what you meant.' Mickey's snarl was quieter this time, but the menace in his voice was greater. He took the first steps round to Jonathan's side of the fire.

Jonathan's heart was thumping. Had he gone too far? He was worried, but he would be damned if anyone was going to spot it, and he would also be damned if he was going to back down from this lout. His eyes widened in feigned surprise at Mickey's reaction, his voice calm and innocent. 'What I said. I don't do much, but it is honest, which is more than I can say about a good number of people, both those in my position, and yours.'

That was not good enough for Rider; he kept coming.

Then the least expected thing happened. Hudson had been so unobtrusive – a reserved man blending into the night, silently absorbing another world brought to him on the words of foreigners – that Jonathan and the others had tended, without malice, to ignore him. But now he stood and blocked Mickey's advance.

He was a small, tubby man whose thick beard gave him an air of distinction, and his bare scalp shone in the fire's light.

Hudson held up his hand, but he did not touch the Englishman. His voice was deep and resonant, and he spoke with deliberate care as if choosing each word and phrase with caution to make sure it was the most suitable. 'Wait please, Mickey. You will solve nothing this way. I want to tell you something. My country is overwhelmed by violence. I see it every day, on my street, on the corner, everywhere. My people are being killed, they are being beaten, their houses are set on fire, even they are set on fire. All the parties, the ANC, the IFP, the PAC, the government, everybody, they are all fighting, everybody is trying to be top dog. But nobody is winning. In fact, everybody is losing. I hate the violence, Mickey.

'When I was a little boy, my father was killed for his pay, only ten shillings. When I started my beer halls, I trod on many toes. I was a threat to the shebeen owners, so they threatened me. When I took no notice they started their dirty tricks, but I ignored them. I kept to myself and tried to make my business work. They threatened me more. I was beaten many times. Once they did this – you see?' His head bent forward and his stubby fingers ran their way down a long, ugly scar which cut a narrow swathe through the band of hair on the back of his scalp. Every person in the group had seen it, but with typical European sensitivity, had been too embarrassed to ask.

Hudson looked up at Rider again. 'They put me in hospital for a long time, Mickey, but it did not stop me. Now I am much more rich than they are. Violence solves nothing. I came here to find some peace, to escape the violence of my people. You and me, I think our paths from the gutter to success are not so different. Please, I myself, I'm asking you, don't let me find more fighting here.'

Mickey did not look straight at the black man, but over his head gave Jonathan a menacing glare and returned to his seat, grumbling to himself.

Everyone else leaned back in their seats or released their breath, not least Jonathan. 'Will you excuse me for a moment?' Outwardly unperturbed by the issue, he rose to his feet and left the firelight.

Although he half expected to find Mickey waiting for him outside the toilets, Jonathan was not surprised to see Gudrun. She stepped up to him, some two inches taller. Those incredible eyes were cold and angry as she stared down at her lover. 'What do you think you're doing, you stupid man? You're provoking him. The tension between you two is making everything terrible. You have everyone on edge, careful not to say the wrong thing. We could be having a lovely time, but it's impossible to ignore this dumb British class war of yours.'

'I didn't start it. He thought he recognised me for something I'm not, someone who is obscenely rich without having to do a day's work to stay that way. I thought I'd confirm it for him. He has a massive chip on his shoulder, and there's nothing I can do which will make that go away, even though he's wrong.'

'I know, but you don't have to pretend to be such a snob. Up till now, you've made him small at every turn, and now you've hinted he's dishonest.'

'Gudrun, love, I can't stand bad-mannered Philistines, a

prime example of which exists right there. I don't know about Iceland, but the road transport business in Britain is tough. There's fierce competition. To start from scratch and become very rich by the time you're Rider's age in that game means Mickey has used some rather underhand tactics. In short, the man's a crook.'

'Maybe you're right about his honesty, but it would help if you didn't say so. Actually, I don't think he's that bad. He's only putting on a front to be the dominant male. If you were to stop retaliating and accept him, I think he'd be quite pleasant.'

'You would have me lie down and accept his goading? I'm sorry, but I can't do that. And you're wrong about his character; his type are only pleasant if it suits them. What would help, though, is if Kathy stopped behaving like a tramp. Wittingly, or unwittingly, her wide eyed admiration is encouraging him. Why don't you have a girl-to-girl chat with Claire and see if she can restrain her friend.'

'This has nothing to do with Kathy. The problem is you and Mickey Rider. He's unapproachable. You, at least, have the brains to control the situation. For the sake of everyone else, would you please try to do that?'

Back at the fireside, Kathy was still sitting within arm's reach of André and Mickey. Her body, however, leaned to the ranger's side and her fingers were stretched out to his knee.

Jonathan took this in. Was Kathy conscious of what she was doing? For if her previous doe-eyed looks at Rider were anything to go by, her night was not going to be spent with André. *She must know it's wrong and could have repercussions, surely?* Jonathan also noticed Mickey smirking at Gudrun, who was looking like thunder.

'Not changed your mind about the scenery?' Mickey sneered.

Gudrun ignored him, and he laughed. Jonathan chose not

to hear. She was right, the situation had to be defused.

Instead of entering the circle, Jonathan stood at the edge. 'Everyone,' he called, 'I have to confess, and I'm sorry. I've been a bit naughty, I'm afraid. I was playing games; I misled you earlier. I'm not super-rich at all, I don't play polo, nor do I have a big estate or huge investments, and I'm not a director of anything other than our little company, which isn't even a company yet.'

He made a gesture to include Gudrun. 'You heard us tell Annette and Armand what we're doing, and that's true. A little while ago, I made a decision on which direction I was going to take my life. I had the choice of running a successful company, marrying the partner's daughter and having kids, or living a life of adventure. I chose the latter route and faced mixed consequences. It's been exciting and dangerous, but I met Gudrun. I have no regrets over my decision.'

Gudrun held up her hand. 'To answer your question, Kathy, we're financing our trips at the moment from Jonathan's small inheritance, which won't last forever. At home, my family breeds Icelandic horses, so I contribute by selling animals as I need to. They are much valued for export from Iceland.'

Jonathan's announcement lifted an uncomfortable blanket off the group. The upper-class toff, one of the super-wealthy, the odd man out, had been replaced by a person at their own level.

Except for Rider. Jonathan had made a fool of him, and his expression was even more grim than before.

Kathy broke the silence, turning to André. 'What I want to know is what happens to us tomorrow if you get bitten by a snake or something?'

André's laugh had a ring of satisfaction to it. Was the fiction of the game ranger and the hunter's daughter filling his mind at that moment?

As if endorsing that thought, André was unable to keep the huskiness out of his voice. '*Ag*, that's not going to happen. But if it did, Sipho will be there, and he knows what to do.'

'But just suppose we were left alone somehow,' Kathy insisted.

'It would be no problem,' said Annette. 'I'm sure Hudson could guide us home.'

The black man shook his head and beamed. 'I'm very sorry, I would be no good. All my life has been in the city. This is the first time I have been outside Jo'burg.' He broke into a laugh, a wheezing *hee, hee* sound, his tubby body rocking forward. Although the reason was not yet apparent, it caused the others to smile in anticipation of his childish joke. 'I only know one end of an elephant from the other because the front tail is longer than the back one.'

7

Gudrun hovered on the brink of sleep. She was trying to understand why the encounter with the rhino had such a profound effect on her. And it was profound. She was in love with the horses on her father's farm in Iceland – she almost dissolved with emotion whenever a foal was born, those delicate little bodies on long, frail legs tottering around in the early hours of their lives. She tended to the horses every day, but never had anything, neither foal nor puppy, ever produced as much instant affection as that ugly prehistoric cow and her calf. Those weak, piggy little eyes were far too low down, level with the horn and surrounded by wrinkles of worry. The great expanse of bare head between them and their active, trumpet-like ears ought to be filled with brain, but somehow they managed to appear, and were, delightfully dumb. Gudrun didn't care; they were special, and she knew they needed protection.

She looked across the hut to Jonathan. He was snuffling in his sleep as he often did. She had thought it was funny the first time she heard him and teased that he sounded like a pig truffling. Now, she threw back her covers and snuck into his bed.

He rolled over. 'Hello you.'

'Hello, you silly, stubborn man.'

The National Parks Board was not in the business of catering for carnal activities. Mickey's bed was narrow and confining, and the heat of their two bodies had dampened the sheets. But after they were sated, Kathy had been too somnolent to care.

Much later, though, she woke with a start. Hell! It would be light in a little while, and they were setting out at dawn.

Mickey was snoring. She slid out of bed and picked up her clothes. Not bothering to put them on, she padded out of the hut with only a tiny squeak from the boards on the stoep. The camp was bathed in a soft brilliance. Every detail stood out as if it were daytime. With a wonderful sense of freedom she stood stark naked and opened her arms to the moon, trousers in one hand, shirt in the other, and let the chilly night air dry her skin. But the scene soon dissolved into blackness, and as the light went so her arms fell to her side. She had witnessed a rare hole in a bank of cloud which otherwise covered the sky. Did it mean the rains were coming? André had said none would fall until September.

Soft night sounds came to her: a scratching in the nearby undergrowth, some weird screech which might be a hyena was not far away, followed by the spine-chilling roar of a lion. The bush was alive. She was fascinated: all those creatures of every shape and size, all busy with their lives throughout the night.

Her mood was shattered by a sudden sound. Having been brought up near an army camp the noise was familiar to her, but she could not believe it, not here. When it occurred a second time, she was horrified. Man had once again intruded and destroyed the natural course of things.

Far in the distance came the rattle of automatic gunfire.

The more experienced of the poachers was smug; he had been right all along. It had been too early to try for the rhino at dusk, the unexpected presence of the tourists had proven that. Now the strangers were gone, heading back to their comfortable camp with its ample food and beer. But there was no time left, it would be dark in minutes and tracking would be impossible for hours yet. Now they were forced to wait for the moon, the timing he had always thought the most wise.

The poachers relaxed in the peace which reigned in the early evening. They knew everything that would happen, because it always happened that way – animals did not change their habits overnight.

The rhino would be thirsty, because it was the time when they drank. As they had done for millions of years, they would make their way to one of the churned, muddy pools when darkness descended on the bush. With their thirst slaked, the cow, with her calf tucked close beside her, would clamber out of the river to begin their night's feed.

The poachers' patience was rewarded when, somewhere around half past two, a bright, distorted sphere rose from behind the low crest of the Lebombo Mountains, giving every rock and tree a long, deep shadow. Climbing higher, its brilliance grew quickly, bathing the bush in a soft, silvery light.

The time was right. The men picked up the rhino spoor at the river's edge and followed it for a short while, until a thin bank of cloud rolled in from the east. Nature's cloak was drawn across the moon, plunging the bush into intermittent darkness. They cursed – only in the odd bright patch would they be able to track, meaning they might not catch up with the rhino until it grew light.

It took them a long time. In this uncertain dimness, not only was it difficult to see the footprints, but they had to move carefully. The rhino would take fright at the slightest sound, long before they could be seen. Likewise, the men heard the beasts before they saw them. The breaking and tearing of twigs, the rumbling of a stomach, the odd shuffle, all were enough to guide them. It was not easy to see a grey hulk amongst grey trees in the dark minutes before dawn, but they found them.

Three of the men spread out to cover a wider area in case the animals were to move and present a different view. The leader, the man to do the killing, crept to the side seeking a better shot, each step slow and silent, a study in care. To snap a twig now would send the rhino snorting into the darkness. She would be lost in the time it took to flick off a safety catch, and they would have to start all over again.

At last he was in position, the cow's whole flank presented to him, her calf well below the level of her heart and out of the way. Good. He was not interested in the calf, it was too small, its horn undeveloped, a mere suggestion of a pinnacle on its nose.

Although their field-craft was excellent, these were unsophisticated and ignorant men. Their knowledge of firearms was limited to loading, pointing and pulling the trigger. The concept of aiming was a science ignored. He fired from the chest, the butt away from his body as if he was frightened of the gun. The automatic weapon seized control of its own affairs, a living thing jumping in his hands. The first few bullets thudded into the solid body, the others sprayed skywards in a harmless arc.

With a piercing snort and a squeal of pain, the cow bolted. With her frantic calf hard at her heels, she charged through the dense thorn bush with the power and noise of a locomotive.

Another man caught a glimpse of the galloping bulk and fired a burst. It was erratic, lasting long after the beast had gone, and ended only when his corroded magazine jammed.

The men did not argue for long. There was no time for recriminations. Minute by minute the greyness lightened. Soon the sun would be up and people in the reserve would start to move.

They picked up the spoor and set off in pursuit. Although they were far behind the rhino, they knew that all they had to do was stick to the trail and they would find her. But even though the cow was zigzagging all over the bush, her general direction was west, towards the camp.

Daylight was not far away when the worst happened for the poachers. The cloud thickened, the breaks in it ceased and, in the hour before dawn, the approaching light withdrew and darkness fell again, forcing them to slow their pace. But time was short, there was so much to do, and they were far too close to the camp for comfort. With every passing moment, the chance of discovery and conflict with the rangers increased.

Injured, frightened and almost blind, the rhino charged through the bush in utter panic, followed by her desperate calf who struggled to keep pace. Soon the shots made themselves felt. One round had struck her rump, but she didn't notice that. Another was in her belly; a terrible fire of pain. The other had punctured her lung. Blood and air were drawn into the chest cavity with each agonising breath. Little by little they filled it, compressing the lung and starving her of precious oxygen at a time when she needed it most.

She did not know which direction she was going in, only that she had to keep moving to protect her baby, to run away from her agony, to escape from whatever dreadful thing had caused it. But she slowed, her energy sapped with every wasted drop of blood. Her legs grew weaker, the strides shorter. The spring was no longer in her step, and once or twice she stumbled. The little calf kept pace with her, right on her heels and terrified in his ignorance.

As the sky lightened, she left the trackers far behind. But traces of her waning strength were becoming apparent: a drag in her footprints and, less easy to see, more frequent drops of blood.

The rhino could go no further. There was no space in her chest, her heart too was restricted, and with weak, ineffectual beats it struggled in vain to keep her alive.

First she stopped and wavered, her great head hanging, her panting short and shallow and spraying a bright red froth which bubbled at her nostrils. Her little one was exhausted and bewildered. A forlorn little figure, he stood and watched as his mother first sank to her knees, then collapsed upright with her legs folded under her. He stared as she tried in vain to keep her head erect, but its weight proved too much and her chin sagged to the ground. Each laboured breath blew a weak puff of dust from beneath her nose. In a short while even that stopped.

The calf could not understand. He tried in vain to wake the only protector he had, nudging her repeatedly. Without her he was doomed, with little hope of lasting out the day in the face of many merciless, hungry predators. He was still leaning against the carcass, weak with grief, when the first humans arrived on the scene.

8

As dawn approached, the tourists assembled round the dying, but still warm, embers of last night's fire for coffee and rusks, which Petros had prepared. The air was fresh, and everyone had some form of warm covering over their shirts. Kathy stood next to Mickey and fingered his hand while they drank.

André was more alert and chirpy than most of the group that early in the morning. He was telling them what was going to happen: how they would walk out and find the rhino cow and calf, and how they would be sure to see other creatures during the morning. They would be out until lunchtime, but how far they would travel would depend on what they saw.

'You won't be disappointed, I—' He stopped in mid sentence and looked away. Swirling his mug around, he tossed the dregs into the ashes. 'Right, let's go.'

Kathy's swallow was involuntary. He'd seen what her hand had been doing. The surprise on his face had been fleeting, instantly replaced with a look of betrayal which burned its way into her. A rare blush of shame coloured her

43

cheeks.

Each tourist had a small backpack with some water and things they did not want to go without: hat, sunglasses and sun cream amongst them. They adopted the same order as the previous evening and followed the ranger out of the camp.

André's pace had Kathy sweating in her jacket where the little pack clung to her shoulders and back. It was fast to begin with, much too fast, and she knew he was taking his anger out on them all because of her. He slowed only after Sipho called out something in Afrikaans.

She was glad of the speed though, the rhythm of exercise helping to drive out her shame. It was Claire, of course, who had pointed out that her treatment of André was despicable. Her friend had even called her a prize bitch, which she knew she deserved.

It might have been acceptable if she had been teasing a world-wise yuppie, but the ranger was a harmless, perhaps naïve, man who in all probability had never experienced such fickleness in the close community in which he lived. She dropped further back in the line, embarrassed and unable to summon the courage to face him and tell him of the shooting – a disastrous omission.

It was a strange noise; Jonathan could not begin to think what animal was making it. He looked at André, but the ranger's puzzled expression was no help. At first it sounded as if something was grunting, but there was also pain, and he detected an infinite sadness in the cries. Sipho showed no signs of recognition either. André held the tourists in a tight group while the tracker crept forward to see what he could find. He was back after a few minutes during which time the visitors had become more and more curious. Dropping to his haunches beside André, he spoke in taut, hushed tones.

Mickey's voice was a loud whisper. 'What is it?'

André's hand flashed up for silence. He shook his head, his lips clamped tight with rage. All semblance of his usual warmth had left his face. He glanced at the tourists one by one. Jonathan met his eyes, but André was staring straight through him. *He's not registering us. What the hell's got into him?*

The ranger shook his head. He appeared to be trying to bring himself under control.

'What's going on?' Mickey said.

'Wait a minute,' André ordered, before remembering they were guests. 'Sorry, I tell you just now.'

He pulled out his portable radio and spoke in a hushed tone. 'Kilo Papa One, this Romeo Two Zero.' He waited: nothing. He repeated his call: nothing. He tried another channel: still nothing. He fiddled with the knobs, but even with the volume up full there was no hint of static from the squelch.

André muttered to himself, his fingers fumbling as he checked the short aerial to see if it was connected. It came off in his hand. He swore in Afrikaans and held the radio out for Jonathan to see the distinct scuff mark on the top corner of the set.

'It been dropped, and there only one *blerry* idiot that done it.'

Armand leaned towards him. 'What is 'appening, André? What is the problem?'

'Silence, please. I tell you just now. But we must get into this donga first.'

The gully closed in on the group as he led them to clamber down its steep sides from which roots and stones protruded. Like a soldier's trench, it offered some protection from whatever danger roamed outside, but did not eliminate the threat. In the drought it was dry, of course, but even so the vegetation was thicker, and the multitude of larger kudu tracks were smothered in places by those of the smaller buck and tiny duiker. This was clearly a favourite feeding spot.

André and Sipho whispered to each other in Afrikaans. Then, before the frustrated tourists knew what was happening, the black man once again used his incredible ability to melt into the bush.

The ranger gathered the tourists around him in a tight huddle, their heads close together, their voices kept low. Jonathan glanced round the group. Like himself, they were all nervous as to what could be wrong. *We're so out of our element.*

'Poachers,' André hissed. 'They've shot the rhino.'

Like a class full of children, the whole group gasped at once.

Gudrun was the first to break the silence which followed. Her eyes were damp, and she was struggling to control her voice. 'Our rhino? The ones we saw yesterday?'

André nodded.

Horrified, she fired questions at him, but he shook his head in reply. 'Did Sipho see them? No? Then he must be wrong; it's not possible. No one could *do* a thing like that.'

Jonathan could think of nothing constructive to say, and everyone else remained speechless, staring at the ranger. Annette turned away from him and hid her face in Armand's shoulder.

Mickey seemed bemused at first. 'They've killed that bloody great thing for its horn? I mean, you read about it, but you're not there. It's … it's far away somewhere. Those bastards are right here, aren't they? We've got to get 'em.'

Both Claire and Kathy jumped at his outburst. 'Keep your voice down,' Claire snapped.

Jonathan said, 'We'd be stupid to try and do anything—'

Mickey turned on him, thrusting his flushed, pugnacious face into Jonathan's like a drill sergeant bullying a recruit.

'And why bloody not? You lot are all the same, as soon as there's a sniff of trouble you run and hide and let some other poor sod take the heat.'

Jonathan retreated a step with a curl to his lip as if there were a bad smell under his nose. To his mind there was only one person in charge of this group, for the simple reason that none of the tourists had any idea how to cope, in what to them was an alien environment.

'It's quite simple,' he said. 'These guys will be armed with Soviet assault rifles – AK47s. Am I not correct, André? There are thousands of them lying around in Mozambique. There's been a war on there for years. It's supposed to be over now, but the country is teeming with bandits and armed gangs. It would be stupid for anyone to tackle them without weapons – even you Mickey.'

Gudrun leaned in to the group, her words forceful. 'Well something's got to be done. We can't let them get away with it. André, you're the expert, what's going to happen now?'

She was the most upset of all of them, but angry too. It was the first glimpse the others would have seen of the steely determination which ran through her. Jonathan had experienced it before – most when she'd been willing to let their would-be assassins die high in the Andes – and recognised its resurgence now. This was another critical situation in which, if he didn't watch and restrain her, her impulsive behaviour might cause problems.

'Gudrun is right,' Armand said, 'We must take some action, this is a terrible thing.'

'*Non, chérie,*' Annette replied. 'Jonathan is right. It is too dangerous, we are not armed, and in any case we are innocents here in the bush. It would be suicide.'

Sensitive to her concern, Armand backed down at once, retreating from the discussion.

It was plain to Jonathan that Mickey was not going to have

all these people discussing what was, in his mind, his decision. But as Rider opened his mouth, it was once again Hudson who stopped him with a raised flat hand.

His words were heavy and slow. 'It would be most unwise to try to apprehend these men. Of all of us, I am the most qualified to speak about violence in my country. Please believe me when I say that they will surely have AKs. In this country the AK47 has become the symbol of death. There are too many about, and there are too many dead people who could have told you there is no defence against this terrible weapon which shoots many bullets. Only André and Sipho have guns. They fire one bullet at a time. You will not try to arrest these men with that on your own, will you André?'

'*Dankie*, Hudson, you are right. In any case,' André said, looking straight at Mickey Rider, '*I'm* the expert. And *I'm* in charge. The poachers are not here now. They must have shot the animal and wounded it. It has run here and died. It was its calf crying that we heard. They will be tracking the mother, and just now they will be here to cut off its horn.'

Armand said, 'But why didn't we 'ear the shooting, was it too far away?'

'*Ja*, most probably. Or else we was asleep. If I'd known, you people would not be here now. I'd have called Skukuza on the radio, and we'd have had some back-up here in a helicopter long before they reached the border. My radio is broken, you saw, so I sent Sipho back to the camp to try anyway. Now, it may be too late, but …'

Jonathan glanced at the others to see how they were reacting. Rider had retreated, the French looked concerned, and, to his inexperienced eye, Hudson had no readable expression. Kathy had her head down, while Claire was staring at her as if she knew something was wrong but did not know what. Gudrun, however, was all vengeance.

André was still talking. 'I wanted to send you all with him, get you out of danger, but you would slow him down. Now I should take you back myself, but I have to see these men. If we don't get them this time, with a bit of luck one day I can identify them. You'll be safe here. I'll be back just now, because they won't be around long. Don't make a noise and don't move from here. Understand? Okay?'

Without a word of dissent, the group of tourists watched the ranger scale the bank and disappear over the lip. It took some time before it dawned on them they had been left on their own.

André found the rhino without difficulty. One glance at the scene – the dead cow, the helpless calf – and the rage within him almost became unmanageable. Somehow he pulled himself together. About forty metres away from the carcass was a dead marula tree, uprooted by some hungry elephant an age ago. It was too close to the rhino for comfort, but there was no other cover. He wormed his way under and behind the trunk so he had a view from beneath it, checked his rifle and eased it into a ready position. He drew dry branches around his outline and, settled, was able to wait and watch the pathetic little calf as it grieved and cried. Tears of anger and pity rolled down his own cheeks.

André had no idea how long it would be before the poachers arrived. He was concerned, because he could not leave the tourists alone for long. In fact, he should not have left them alone at all.

Without warning, four men appeared on the far side of the rhino, their need for extreme caution now over. After a few minutes of hectic, bloody work, they would be running for the border with their grisly prize.

A hard, tight pack of hair-like fibres growing from below the skin, the rhino's horn could be slashed free with an axe. But to do that the poachers were going to have to distract the calf, for he would defend his mother's body to the end.

André was confident they wouldn't shoot the baby – they were too close to the camp and, at the sound, they'd have trackers and a helicopter on their tails. There would be little chance of escape.

The calf whirled round at the men's approach, struggling to focus his myopic eyes on the threat. André watched, sickened, as the calf, with a shrill squeal of rage, charged at a fuzzy image which moved somewhere ahead of him. He might only have been a baby, but the ground still trembled beneath his feet. The man leapt clear. The calf spun to follow and the dust rose in a thick cloud around him. Another image, half formed, was by his mother. He turned on that, but it too vanished from his sight, leaving him panting and bewildered.

André's tears ran unchecked; there would be only one end to this pitiful spectacle.

The calf stood at his mother's head. He charged a few steps at a man then, as he was taunted from a different angle, switched to another blurry shape. Somehow he managed to prevent anyone from coming too close. But after the long chase he was tiring. The men dodged him with ease and, laughing, they began a cruel, teasing and deadly game of blind man's bluff.

André prayed for them to finish it. This brutal sport had gone on long enough, and time was running out for the poachers. He had seen them, he could identify them again, but he was too close to move. They would spot him immediately; he had to wait until it was all over. As Hudson had said, their AKs fired many bullets. He could only fire one.

Three of the bastards were to the calf's front. Poor little guy couldn't count; pitiful creature couldn't see the fourth leave the group and circle round to the other side of the carcass.

The panga rose high and fast. To André it was a mere glint

in the early-morning light, falling with tremendous power straight across the calf's left hamstring. His cry of pain and shock rang through the bush. He tried to turn on this new threat but his leg was useless. The man was so close he must have had a clear view of him, the panga raised again. The second blow immobilised him and, amid his childish squeals of agony, the other men came into focus.

André retched, but somehow he managed to swallow his vomit.

9

André had only been gone for ten minutes when Mickey's patience ran out. 'Where the hell has he got to?' He jumped to his feet and stomped up and down the short stretch of donga. Unlike the others, who had all heeded the advice to wear neutral clothing, he had on the same ghastly colour combination he had worn the previous night. Legs which had never seen the sun bulged out the bottom; powerful white supports set in the brown foundation of his red-laced boots.

Like everyone else, Jonathan tried hard to ignore him. The exception was a nervous Kathy, who tried to calm him with soothing words. 'It's too soon, surely. He must be all right, he knows what he's doing.'

'No it's not too bloody soon,' Mickey snapped. 'You stick to what you're so good at, darling, and let men take care of the action.'

Kathy blushed and kicked at the dust. Claire was glaring at her, but she kept her head down. The play escaped neither Jonathan nor Gudrun. He looked at her. She shrugged, but he could tell she shared his suspicions.

To Jonathan, Rider was insufferable. 'Do try to talk quietly,' he said in a hushed tone. 'In fact, *if* you give it some thought, it's highly unlikely he'd be back already. Say five minutes to reach the rhino if he sneaks up on the kill, and the same time to return, then you have to add whatever is necessary for him to spy on them. And of course we don't even know if the poachers have reached here yet.'

Mickey stopped pacing and swung round. Aggression, it appeared, was his only way of relieving tension. But Annette smiled encouragement at him while indicating her agreement with Jonathan, and Armand said. 'We cannot know 'ow long he will be. It is better to relax, Mickey, no?'

For a while he tried, but could not stop marching about. After another five minutes he broke off a few small branches, then tucked bits of dry grass into his hatband. 'I've had it. Poor bugger's probably in need of help and we're sitting here like bleeding stuffed ducks. To hell with it, I'm off to see what's going on. The rest of you had better stay put.'

'Why don't you do what the expert told you to do and remain here? You might compromise our position by doing something he knows nothing about.' Jonathan's words encouraged a murmured chorus of support from the others.

'Why don't you find the guts to do something instead of sitting here pretending you know everything? You're too young and too weak. I've got the experience, and I've got the guts.'

Jonathan shook his head, whispering to Gudrun, 'He certainly enjoys the attention, even if it's not the type he wants.'

Armand and Hudson tried to explain the situation, without implying he was being stupid. 'Sipho will be back in camp by now, Mickey. 'Elp will come soon.'

Mickey snubbed them.

Kathy clutched at his arm. 'Mickey, it's too dangerous.'

He pulled away from her, and she again blushed and

looked hurt.

Mickey, though, seemed to grow in stature, proud and unmoved.

'God, look at him. He's a monument to heroism, sword raised to the heavens and surrounded by a throng of weeping bare-breasted women reaching up to him, beseeching him not to place himself in danger,' Jonathan said.

Gudrun sniggered.

'I'm going and that's that,' Mickey announced. 'If I'm not back in half an hour, you men had better take the girls back to camp.'

'Ah, a celluloid hero's immortal lines.'

'What did you say?' Mickey was already half way up the bank. One hand held on to a root, the muscles of his forearm bulging, while the other gripped loose branches. His glare threatened from the shade of his hat, although the few bits of grass he'd stuffed in the headband made him seem more comical than dangerous.

'I said, watch out for lions.'

'It's not lions you'd better watch out for, mate.'

At about the same time that Mickey made his fateful decision, Sipho reached the camp. He had run all the way using the long, easy stride which could support him at that pace for hours. The sweat streamed off his skin and soaked his clothing, not only in isolated patches under the arms or down the back, but right through. It was nothing. His only concern was to help André catch these Mozambicans.

Sipho knew the money those men would receive for the horn was nothing compared to what others further down the line would gain. That was the stupidity. The poachers destroyed the environment on which the entire tourist industry relied, which meant they were threatening the livelihood of men like him and Petros. Not to mention the lives of the rhinos and the elephants. They were bad men and they had to be punished for this waste.

As Sipho neared the camp, he paused and wiped the sweat from his face. Above the sound of his panting, the game-viewer's engine sprang into life. '*No!* Petros!' he screamed and sprinted up the hill. Reverse was engaged with a crunch. The engine roared and tyres ground the hard, packed dirt. The vehicle and its radio disappeared, leaving him alone in the camp.

Sipho staggered into the circle of huts in time to see nothing of the departing truck but the cloud of dust which hung between the trees over the track. That final spurt had left him gasping. While he recovered his breath, he glanced around the kitchen. Why had Petros left? Where had he gone? In the rubbish were the remains of an entire tray of eggs and a split plastic milk bottle. Not so important perhaps, but Sipho knew it was another dent in Petros's pride. Everyone knew how clumsy he was, it was a joke amongst all the rangers, black and white: 'Hey Petros, what have you broken today?'

This time it was the shelf in the gas refrigerator. There was nothing for the guests to eat for lunch or any other meal, today or tomorrow. So an embarrassed Petros must have gone for supplies from the tea room at Tshokwane, six kilometres away. What with the travelling and the buying and the talking that Petros would do, he would take a minimum of an hour. But he knew the trailists would not be back in camp for at least another ninety minutes yet, so he could afford to delay his return, especially if he got chatting to Elias. Those two! Sipho had long advocated that the chief ranger should make a rule to stop them talking to each other forever.

Sipho sank several large glasses of water while he thought out a plan. Time was critical, and the best thing was for him to run to the road and stop a car which would either take him to Tshokwane or intercept Petros – anything to reach a radio. He slung his rifle over his shoulder and loped up the track towards the main road.

The task at hand was butchery. Pangas appeared, the guns tossed to one side. André curbed his revulsion and nausea at what was happening. At that moment he was the only man with a firearm; he could arrest the bastards. But first he had to crawl out of his hiding place under the log to take a dominating position. The poachers were only a step, a second from their weapons. With great care, he made his first shift sideways.

He froze. Not because the poachers saw him, but because of the apparition which popped out from between the bushes. The hat stuffed with grass, the ruddy face beneath and that dreadful loud shirt, as incongruous as a marula in the Arctic and in no way hidden behind the pathetic array of twigs held in Mickey's hand.

The bloody fool was going to ruin everything. André was still hidden from the poachers and not ready to move. He hissed at the tourist and waved him away. Mickey saw him at once and grinned with relief, misinterpreted the signal and crawled forward, totally exposed. Two metres separated them.

The Mozambicans saw him. One moved fast. His back to André, who was still beneath the marula, his panga hovered over Mickey's throat. André saw Rider freeze but for a light, uncontrollable tremble in his knees.

André rose off the ground, his safety catch clicking off. A warning shout came from the other poachers. But the panga was already carving a wide arc as the man spun round with a blind swipe at the enemy behind. It hit André in a level slash across his chest, slicing between the ribs and thudding to a stop in his breastbone. The blow knocked him over, and the blade's tip sliced into his heart.

Jonathan fidgeted, strode up and down the short space in the donga, plucked twigs and snapped them in two, before sitting again. Armand did the same thing until Annette called him to her. The rest of them were silent, each keeping to their own thoughts, except for the odd whisper between couples. Claire and Kathy were sitting close together, one calm, the other on the verge of panic. Only Hudson kept still and quiet.

Jonathan checked his watch for the umpteenth time. A noise, a rustle. He and Gudrun glanced at each other and up at the rim. Mickey burst out from behind a bush and jumped down into the gully. He landed halfway down the slope and fell.

'They've killed him,' he jabbered from the ground. '*Jesus!* He's cut in two. Blood all over the place. Just like that, one bloody great swipe and he's gone. *Jesus!* They almost got me too. I ran for my life. We've got to get out of here. They'll be after us.' He scrambled to his feet and grabbed hold of the nearest arm, Armand's.

The Frenchman's hand was shaking under Mickey's trembling grip.

'I saw it, right in front of my bleeding eyes. *Jesus!*'

For a few seconds, no one appeared to believe him. They were all gaping, stunned into silence. Jonathan put his arm around Gudrun, and she around him. He looked to see how she was taking the news. Her lips were set in a thin straight line, her eyes flinty. Anger had replaced her shock, and she was ready to fight.

Annette's crying broke the spell, and suddenly they were all babbling at once.

They turned to Hudson: this South African must know what to do. He would talk to these poachers and reason with them, black man to black man. But Hudson seemed to shrink before them. A cloak of depression had fallen over him. He looked as if he wasn't conscious.

'Hudson?' Jonathan said.

'Is there no escape from the violence, even here? A good man is killed by the cut of a panga. His body is split open to the sun and the flies. What is new in that, I ask you? Only the place, my friends. I thought I was used to it, because it is something that happens every night in the townships. But not here. Man should not kill man in this reserve. It should be a place of peace. There is no escape from violence.'

Jonathan held his own wild feelings in check and tried to inject some calm into the others. 'Listen everybody, we're behaving like chickens with a fox in the run. The buggers are not here yet, so we should take advantage of that, stop talking and get the hell out of here while we still can.'

Armand released Annette. '*Oui*. Let's go.'

Kathy's voice was tremulous. 'Which way? We can't see anything down here. Which way's the camp?'

There was a chorus of, 'That way,' from the group, but the fingers all pointed in different directions. Jonathan was about to take control when Armand, the most practical of them, said, 'Please follow me. The important thing is to get away from here, we can find the camp later.'

It was what Jonathan was going to say, but he decided to bow to Armand's greater age and experience and let him lead. The confidence in the Frenchman's voice sounded more than anyone else could summon, so they did as they were told. Jonathan ushered the women ahead of him, intending to guard the rear, although what he effect he would have there he had no idea. For a moment his glance met Gudrun's, and a flash of mutual support passed between them.

Armand had reached the lip of the donga. Annette, behind him, was halfway up the slope and the others beginning the scramble when two ragged-looking men appeared on the opposite side.

10

Gudrun was used to guns. Like many Icelanders, her father had a small selection for hunting, and he had taught her how they should be handled. She watched with increasing concern as the poachers waved their assault rifles about with a dangerous carelessness. The weapons, a finger curled around each trigger, tracked across the tourists, pointed east repeatedly, aimed at the sky or dangled towards the ground.

Hudson shook his head as if to rid himself of a memory. 'They want us to go with them.' His voice was hoarse; he cleared his throat. 'We should do what they want, it is not wise to disobey.'

The group drew closer together like sheep. Will that give us more protection?

But there was no time to think, no time for the fear and panic to subside. Gun barrels jabbed at their flesh. Incomprehensible commands were spat at them in harsh tones, the voices kept low. One of the men led the way, the other hustled them into line and pushed them forward. The pace was fierce. Kathy, with her short legs, had to trot to keep up. Within a couple of minutes they were at the kill.

The pathetic grey hulk of the beast dominated the scene ahead of Gudrun. Its forelegs were folded beneath it. Its ears, once upright trumpets, had now sagged flat like handlebars on the heavy head. Blood still oozed from its nostrils to form a sticky pool too viscous to penetrate the dusty soil. At its tail lay her baby. He was a pitiful sight, on his side, his hind legs cut above the hock. Brutal wounds to his neck had bled out to the ground.

Two men stood, one on either side of the mother's head, each with a panga dangling from his hand. They had paused in their hacking and were staring, curious of the white strangers. But they were in a hurry – every moment of delay brought discovery a step closer. They rushed on with their crude butchery, the smaller rear horn already chopped clear.

Gudrun gaped at the scene. It was too far-fetched, too ghastly to contemplate. She winced as each panga strike ended in a solid thump and a spray of blood. She was trembling, not from shock, but from rage.

She glanced at the others: Claire and Annette were overwhelmed with horror, dumbfounded and, like her, unable to believe what they were witnessing. Kathy's look was blank. Her words were a hoarse whisper. 'Where's André?'

Mickey pointed in the direction of the dead tree, and looked away. His voice sounded like hers. 'There.' It would be the last thing he said for a long time.

Kathy took a few hesitant steps past Gudrun towards the ranger. The waxen pallor of death had already settled on him. His tan had turned a sickly yellow. All the blood in his veins had drained onto the ground and mingled with the dust in a dark pool.

Gudrun saw Kathy was swaying, saw her eyes roll back. She jumped forward. A poacher raised his gun at her. She ignored him, and in two strides had an arm beneath Kathy's.

Claire joined her. Together they lowered her to the ground.

Annette, who everyone had assumed to be reliant on Armand, who could do nothing without him, rushed over to help. 'It is the heat and the shock. It is too much for her.'

While Claire tended to her friend, Gudrun, with a mixture of horror and anger, turned to watch the poachers work. Comprehension of this brutality was impossible. For a while she stared at the huge carcass. A sack lay at the rhino's snout. It could only be for one thing, and it drew her like a magnet. In a daze, she walked forward to the mutilated head and reached down, as if to feel a loved one for the last time. The skin felt as it looked: tough and coarse and dusty. The front horn had been freed, and the butchers had finished. They stood, weapons dangling from their hands, and watched her with suspicion.

Her reverie broke. She stepped away and reached for the sack. Guns were raised. She took no notice. Was this what it was all about? These hard, shiny, pointed horns which, now chopped from the skull with careless brutal hacks, had lost all their appeal? Once marks of character, they were now inanimate, rendered impotent by some distant human who had paid to have this great beast destroyed. In God's name, why?

She lifted the sack, expecting a weight, but was surprised how light it seemed, perhaps four and a half kilos.

She was seized by an enormous will. The horns were the last remains of the rhino, *her* rhino. Nothing was going to separate them from her without her consent. It was the least she could do; an act on behalf of all compassionate humans to beg forgiveness for the wrongs of their kind.

The poachers had lowered their guns and only cast the odd glance in her direction. There was nothing she could do, she could not steal the horns from them, and she could not escape without being shot.

They babbled amongst themselves in an argument between the older man and the three younger ones. They kept looking at Hudson.

'You speak their language?' Annette said.

'Yes, they are Tsonga people. I don't understand perfectly, but better than I will let them think.'

Claire nodded. 'Smart move.'

The poachers reached agreement and called Hudson over. The three youths all jabbered at him at once. His apparent difficulty in understanding had them edgy. One thrust his chin forward, one jabbed fingers at him, and one fingered his rifle. The older man silenced the others and explained. Whatever he said caused Hudson to shake his head in refusal. One of the young men rammed his gun at Hudson's ample belly. The black man rubbed the spot and turned to the rest of the group. 'They're going to take us with them.'

Annette clutched her husband's arm. He was open mouthed. 'You mean we are being kidnapped?'

'But why? What good can it do them?' Claire said.

Armand shrugged. 'Ransom perhaps? We are witnesses, are we not?'

Gudrun studied Hudson. He had a look of resignation about him, resignation mixed with fear, which came out in his weary reply. 'From what I understand, the older man wanted to leave us here, but the young ones, they want to use us as shields in case the rangers catch up with them. They spoke about ransom after they reach their village, as a bonus.'

'Hudson,' Armand said, 'do they want us to go with them only to the border, or all the way to their village in Mozambique? There will be terrible consequences.'

'Yes, I think that is what they want to do, to go all the way.'

Gudrun sought out Jonathan. What were the ramifications of being kidnapped, and how might they affect her keeping the horns?

* * *

The consequences of being taken hostage dawned on them. They murmured to one another, seeking reassurance and trying to be optimistic without any real foundation. Kathy had come round but was sitting on the ground, shaking her head and taking no part the discussion.

Jonathan was impatient for a decision, some action which would lead to a conclusion of this nightmare. Mickey remained silent. Jonathan was itching to take control, but worried that if he opened his mouth the man would snap out of his shocked state and resist, causing more unnecessary conflict at a time when they needed to stick together.

'Let's keep calm and listen to Armand,' said Jonathan in a steady tone. 'He has the most experience.'

Armand shot him a look of appreciation, while the others stopped their chatter and turned their attention to the Frenchman. 'If they force us across the border it will be most serious. There is always fighting over there. There are bandits and renegade soldiers and terrorists. And they're all hungry and 'ave no money.'

'What should we do, *chérie*?' Annette had an arm on his shoulder. She was so trusting in him, so confident he could solve this problem.

'We should not argue with them now. Let us go with them to the fence and then insist they let us go. If we get a chance, it will be at the border. André told us the army patrols the fence, looking for refugees. With luck they will be close.'

That was common sense. Jonathan said, 'I think their main concern is to get out of the park as soon as possible, they're in danger here. They might well let us go once we reach the border. After all, we'll only be a hindrance to them in Mozambique. What would they do with us?'

'*C'est possible*, but we cannot rely on that. There was talk of ransom later. It is important we delay them as much as we can at the fence. Remember, Sipho will 'ave made contact with Skukuza by now. It will not be long before 'elp arrives in a 'elicopter.'

Mickey came to life. 'I reckon we should tell them where to stuff it right now,' he muttered, but there was little enthusiasm in his voice. Jonathan gave him a contemptuous look. Mickey was saying something to keep up appearances, knowing no one would endorse it. No one did.

Hudson's attention flicked from one speaker to another. 'Be careful, please. They have AKs, and they are not trained soldiers, so they are very dangerous. I don't think they are murderers, it is not in their eyes. But they are frightened, they want to be safe in their own country. If anyone makes them too angry, they will react badly.'

It did not take long to get moving.

Flies had already swarmed to the scene, buzzing noisily around their heads. The poachers pushed the tourists into a line with sticky, bloodied hands. Jonathan stood close to Gudrun. She was clutching the sack and might need his support. One of the men tried to rip it from her, but she held on and pushed him off. Surprised, he stumbled and almost lost his balance. His panga rose. No woman should do that.

Jonathan stepped forward. An AK was at his chest. He stopped.

Gudrun stood her ground, tall and commanding. She said nothing, but under her piercing glare the man hesitated.

The tourists stood immobilised, knowing the slightest movement could trigger the wrong reaction. To Jonathan, Gudrun was a hair's breadth from being carved in two. The young white woman and the black hunter with his panga stared each other down. Time dragged.

One of the other poachers laughed, shattering the tense silence and defusing the situation.

The panga was lowered and the youth turned away, his

face brimming with resentment .

Jonathan relaxed. '*Whew!* That was bloody brave, but it was also bloody silly. You've made your point. Now let me carry it for you, you've too much weight there.'

'*No*,' she said, then touched his hand. 'Thank you, *Sœti*, but this is mine.'

After that, the poachers did not seem to mind her taking their prize possession. Jonathan was surprised, but guessed it saved one of them the effort.

Again the pace was fast. The hunters kept prodding them on with gun barrels and spitting out the same words over and over again: *hurry, hurry*. Although there was no direct sun, the day's heat was building fast. With the exercise, sweat broke from their pores and turned to rivulets within seconds. Only Armand appeared comfortable, but he was a runner, and more fit than the others.

Mickey had been quiet for an unusually long time. André's brutal killing had to have affected him much more than he would admit. He must have been terrified after that single vicious slash. It was bad enough for Jonathan to see the end result; would witnessing the actual killing have affected him as it did Mickey? Whatever, it was satisfying to know the thug had a weak spot and was not as tough as he made out.

Time passed, and Mickey was unable to keep quiet for long. As if there was security in conversation he said, 'Bloody lions are going to smell us, then what's going to happen? You all heard what André told us about the lion what charged the tourists from a hundred metres and had to be shot. It was bloody unusual, he said, probably disturbed by the bloody drought.' His voice went up an octave. 'What are we going to do about a charging bloody lion?'

Jonathan couldn't resist. 'Simple,' he said. 'Call it "pussy", feed it a biscuit and scratch its ear. They're rather partial to that, I understand.'

Gudrun hit him on the arm to stop further inflammatory words, but the lack of a reply from Mickey was more menacing than any angry outburst.

From deep amongst the trees it was impossible to see far ahead, but they began to climb a gentle slope and the view improved. These were the Lebombo Mountains. The border could not be far away now, and Jonathan refused to think any further ahead than that. The fence was where they were going to stop, it was where they were going to delay the poachers by any means possible. Every minute could make a difference, but one thing was certain: if they went through the fence, all hope of rescue was futile.

Without warning, the leader stopped. The other poachers forced the tourists into a tight group and squatted around them, brandishing their guns with their usual unnerving lack of care.

'He has gone to check the fence line is clear,' Hudson whispered. 'I think these men are very scared of the rangers and the army. We should be careful what we do, they might explode with great ease.'

Jonathan had a sudden vision of the hunters bursting at random around them … pop, pop, pop. But to smile would be to mock. Instead, he winced as one of the men gave Hudson a vicious kick in the back and hissed angry words at him.

Every one of them was in a state of shock. And it was the intrinsic violence of these men which kept them there. The man could have merely told Hudson to keep quiet, so why did he have to kick him so hard? Why did he have to kick him at all? Hudson's warning had not been empty words.

The cloud cover was breaking apart, the sun driving its way through, burning off whatever moisture had settled overnight and heating up the land again with no sign of real relief. The group waited, barely moving, hoping to cool, for there was hardly a breath of wind.

Jonathan explored his immediate surroundings: the khaki grass was warm to the touch, the soil collapsed to dust when kicked, and fragile desiccated leaves crackled in his fingers. He gave vicious, frequent and futile swats to the irritating host of flies which aimed to suck the sweat around his eyes and mouth.

The scout returned. The army was nowhere to be seen, and the hunters became more cheerful. They hustled the group to their feet and into line before setting another rapid pace to the border.

The tourists' first hope of rescue had evaporated. Even so, they strained to hear the sound of a helicopter. Surely enough time had passed for the authorities to react?

A strip of cleared ground ran across their path. In its middle lay a narrow, sandy track. The Kruger Park officials used it for maintenance, and the army used it to patrol the border. On its far side rose an ordinary high game fence. Jonathan was surprised – he had expected something more grand to mark an international boundary.

The older man was working on the fence, kneeling with his back to them and parting previously cut wires to create a space large enough to pass through. His sandals were made from car tyres which still had a good tread. Pointless thought: *What make are they? Michelin, Dunlop, Firestone?*

Most of them were straining their ears for sounds of rescue. Something was needed to lighten the mood. 'They should have names.' Jonathan said, pointing to the old man's sandals. 'He's Retread.'

Annette was relieved at some abstract conversation. She smiled for the first time in ages and asked, 'Why *re*-tread?'.

'Well, the old soul has obviously been around too long to be original.'

Gudrun sniggered. Before she met Jonathan, she would not

have understood the subtlety in English, but he was full of such nonsense, and she picked up most of his silly jokes. This was the weak humour of those under stress, like soldiers joking before a battle, hiding their fear behind a screen of bravado. She pointed at a young man with torn shorts. 'He's Tatty Pants.'

'And he's Red Eyes,' Armand said.

Mickey grunted and sneered something under his breath.

Hudson glanced from one person to another as they spoke. 'I could tell you other names, but you would not understand.'

Claire's lips twitched with amusement. 'The last one has thick, matted hair as if he's just woken up. It has grass in it. Let's call him Jungly.'

Armand became serious, tugging at Hudson's sleeve. 'Now is the time, Hudson. You must tell them we are not going to Mozambique. We 'ave done what they wanted, we 'ave ensured their safety until they get out of the park, but we are not going further.'

'I must tell you, I think this is a very dangerous course of action, Armand. You don't know these men like I do, they are very excited and can be violent. It is better not to provoke them. We will be all right when we get to their village and they calm down. But I will do it. I am very frightened, but I will do it.'

Red Eyes said something, which Hudson translated. 'We are to take off our packs and pass them through the fence to Retread. Quickly, please.'

'Tell 'em to fuck off, Hudson,' Mickey growled after his long absence from the front line. 'We need to show 'em we won't take any shit.'

'Don't, Hudson, please,' Jonathan exclaimed. 'That will only antagonise them. I think they're going to let us go, anyway. I thought they would. They only want our stuff.'

The others seized on that hope and eagerly shed their

backpacks.

'Don't ever override my orders, you. If we didn't have opposition right now, you'd be in deep shit.'

'I wouldn't become too confident if I were you, Rider,' Jonathan reminded him. 'We still have to walk back past the lions with no protection.'

One by one the packs were passed through the fence. Jungly was losing his temper, gesticulating at Gudrun with his weapon.

Hudson's voice betrayed his nervousness. 'He says you must throw the horn through.'

Gudrun fixed her cold stare on the poacher and stuck her chin out. 'No.'

Jonathan gritted his teeth.

Claire touched the Icelander's arm. 'But you must, Gudrun. It's theirs now, there is nothing we can do about it. They hold all the cards.'

'I am not letting go of this horn unless it goes back into the park. It's not theirs, they killed the owner and stole it.'

Everyone crowded round her.

'*Chérie*, it is only a 'orn,' said Annette.

'It is too late, the rhino's already dead,' Armand said.

Mickey chipped in. 'You're mucking with our lives.'

'I said *no!*' she snapped at them, but her eyes never left the poacher. She was clutching the sack to her chest with both arms. 'I'm not giving in to these … these savages. We owe *so much*. The least I can do is stop them having their trophy.'

Jonathan had remained silent. He was proud of her, standing a good half a head above everyone except him and radiating defiance, but he had to calm her down. 'Love, please think of the rest of us. They could kill us all if they start with you. And I don't want to lose you, I love you too much.'

Gudrun turned her head from Jungly for the first time and

glanced at her man. For a second her look softened, reflecting his sentiment back to him before the determination returned.

Jungly demanded to know what was going on. Red Eyes moved closer. Their mood, buoyant and tolerant since they had been at the fence, was turning ugly again.

Kathy came to life. She had said nothing since the scene of the killing. She had fallen into line and walked and trotted along, as if consumed by her thoughts. But now she grabbed Claire's hand and pulled her so the two of them stood between Gudrun and the poachers.

But the hunters were not westerners. They did not like being challenged by a woman, and would not hesitate to use violence on females. Red Eyes grabbed Kathy by the hair and yanked her away. She screamed. Jungly reached for the horn. Gudrun backed away from him. He hit her with a massive swipe across the cheek and wrenched at the sack. She fell but kept her hold.

Jonathan leapt forward. 'Leave her!' he shouted and, threw a punch at Jungly. He missed. Red Eyes' wooden rifle butt swung into his stomach with vicious force. The air went out of him. He doubled over with a groan and collapsed.

Together, Jungly and Tatty Pants picked up Gudrun and tossed her through the fence, still holding fast to her sack. Retread stood over her and jabbed his rifle at her chest.

Armand kept his head. He said to Hudson, 'Tell them to stop this. They can 'ave the 'orn, but we are not going with them. Tell them to send Gudrun back to this side or there will be an international incident.'

'They won't understand, Armand, and they won't care. They think only of instant rewards, not the consequences. To them, we are stealing their livelihood.' But Hudson turned to Red Eyes anyway and spoke rapidly.

The poacher listened for a moment. Without warning, he swung his rifle at Hudson's face. It was a glancing blow which only split the skin, but the chubby businessman fell back onto his bottom. His face took on a vacant look, as if he had escaped to another place, far from the trouble. After a long pause, he appeared to come back to reality again. 'We cannot argue any more, we are to go with them. Our fate is sealed.' He pointed at Gudrun, alone in Mozambique with an armed man.

She had stood, the gun now pointing at her temple. Jonathan saw that a red weal had already risen on her left cheek-bone and a few tears of pain trickled down beside her nose. But her chin was still thrust forward, and she was quivering with rage, her fingers white where she gripped the sack.

'*Ecoutez*! Listen!' Annette's voice radiated hope and excitement. 'A 'elicopter.'

The sound was faint, fading occasionally, then stronger and continuous, a distant throbbing beat reverberating through the bush. Everyone, especially the poachers, were concentrating on the sound. 'There it is.' Annette jumped with eagerness and pointed. 'Down in the valley, they 'ave seen the rhino.'

The helicopter was difficult to spot so far away, but she had keen sight. At one point it glinted in a brief patch of sunlight, and they heard the change of beat as it circled.

The poachers jabbered at each other, but did not insist on moving. They must have thought there was plenty of time for the party to pass through the fence and could afford to indulge in the fascination of staring into the face of the enemy for a little while longer.

The sound died as the machine landed. 'Don't worry,' Armand said, 'they will soon realise what 'as 'appened and come after us.'

'They can do nothing when we're over there,' Mickey said. 'I'm not going, I'm staying here.'

'Gudrun is that side, we can't leave her,' Claire pointed out.

'She brought that on herself. Lover-boy can stay with her if he's got the guts.'

'You are despicable!'

'Stop it, *mes amis! C'est trés* important that we stick together.'

Within moments the machine-gun beat of the helicopter rotor reverberated through the hills again. It was flying low, just above the trees, hard to spot, heading straight for the fence a little south of where they stood. In two minutes it would be with them, dropping off men for the rescue.

The poachers did not seem to appreciate the speed of the machine – they did nothing but argue as their time slipped away. It appeared as if Retread, the oldest, wanted to avoid trouble and let the foreigners go. Tatty Pants was undecided, but the other two were adamant over holding the prisoners. The tourists held their breath; another minute was all they needed.

The percussive beat was growing louder and louder, but the machine was going too far south. It saw them, banked and was now head-on.

That galvanised the poachers into action. They stopped arguing and erupted in a flurry of activity, pushing, shoving, hitting and shouting threats. Somehow they forced the rest of the group into Mozambique on their bellies.

Led by Kathy, who went straight to Gudrun, the tourists scrambled through the narrow gap as the helicopter thundered overhead. Tense faces stared down at them as the machine orbited in a tight turn before landing.

With Gudrun close beside him, her hand on his arm, Jonathan stared up at the circling helicopter, knowing an aircraft cannot land on foreign soil without permission. Never mind that the poachers had also transgressed a border, for some obscure reason an aircraft would create a far more serious incident. That must have been a trivial fact in the minds of the angry rangers, who would love to take revenge, even if it meant a cross-border raid.

What did stop the rangers was the poachers standing in full view with their assault rifles pointed at innocent heads.

They had not moved from the fence. Gudrun was almost within reach of it, and she still held the sack. The helicopter was going to land on the track. It was still banked but was slowing and descending.

Gudrun was up to something. It could only be one thing. Jonathan gave her a subtle look of confidence, trying to lend her strength. Releasing her arm and moving away to give her space, he hissed, 'Ready?'

At some point the poachers' nerve would run out, and they would no longer have the courage to stand and watch. In their minds, if they stayed within reach, the rangers would attack. He was right. It began with shouting and shoving. The tourists were to be herded away.

More seconds of delay would ruin Gudrun's plan. Jonathan shouted, 'Now!'

With all her strength, she hurled the sack as high and far as she could, back over the fence. But it was a throw with no preparatory swing – she couldn't make one without alerting their captors – so it was straight from a standing position. The sack was too heavy and lacked momentum. It snagged on the top strand of wire, whipped over and dumped the larger horn on the ground just inside the park, touching the fence but some six or seven metres from the hole. The sack with the other horn thumped down beside it.

Three seconds of stunned inactivity slowed to a minute. Another blow was going to be dealt. Jonathan stepped between Red Eyes and Gudrun. Armand saw the danger too; he pushed Annette aside and joined the Englishman in staring down the poacher.

The helicopter was about three metres from touch-down. Dust was already billowing away from it and particles of sand lashed and stung exposed flesh. It was Jungly who reacted. With unbelievable speed and agility he dived head first through the fence and sprinted for the horns. He grabbed the sack in one hand and the large horn in the other. There was no time to put the two together, and he was back at the hole and had scrambled through with the speed of a mongoose by the time the first man had jumped from the helicopter.

The rangers were shouting in English, 'Are you all right?' and, 'Don't worry, we'll get you out. Be patient.'

Hudson translated their Tsonga, as they addressed the poachers. 'Take the horn, but let the people go. If you don't there'll be big trouble. We'll tell the government, and the army will kill you when they rescue these people.'

The Mozambicans would not reply. Their nerves were obvious. Tatty Pants and Retread were hedging over releasing the hostages. But Red Eyes was determined, and Jungly was ignoring them. He had already stuffed the horn back into the bag, and from his pocket now produced a length of orange plastic string which he secured round the neck of the material. He snatched Gudrun's hand and tied the sack to her wrist, checked the knot and, pulling her close, gave her a menacing glare. The disgust on her face was clear. She wrinkled her nose and grumbled at his stench of stale sweat and woodsmoke.

Glancing back, he had a final picture of the rangers standing at the fence, helpless, as the group were forced further into foreign territory.

The helicopter was soon airborne again. The kidnappers and their hostages stopped at the sound and turned to watch the machine fly back to the dead rhino and André's body, which would have to be taken to camp as soon as possible to keep it from scavengers.

Uncertainty over the future was now more prominent after the short-lived optimism of having a rescue within touching distance.

They've gone. We've been abandoned to head into a vacuum, into the unknown.

The poachers abruptly broke into simultaneous laughter. The tension burst from them. They had beaten the powerful South Africans with their fancy flying machine; they had faced them down and won. This was a triumph indeed, one which was going to be talked about for many years.

Whatever slate of grievances they had against the foreigners appeared to have been wiped clean. They relived Gudrun's tossing of the sack over the fence. Tatty Pants did a fair imitation of her poor throw, and Red Eyes dived headlong through an imaginary hole in the wire. He pretended to fumble and panic, before racing back to the group on all fours like a baboon, while Retread made ridiculous chopper noises. Jungly was tottering around, bent over with laughter.

'What's worrying,' said Jonathan, 'is the speed at which their mood changes. It's good now, but what will it take for it to turn ugly again? They're volatile.'

Hudson took a deep breath of relief. 'You are right. There is no more danger for now. These men are happy and safe. We can relax, but it would be unwise to cause any more trouble.'

'*Oui*,' said Armand, 'but what is going to 'appen to us? It will be a long time before the authorities can organise our release. Ask them, Hudson, please, and try and persuade them that we will speak well of them if they take us back to the border today.'

'Yes, I'm sure it is safe now,' said Annette, and reached out a supporting hand to the tubby African.

'And tell 'em we'll bring the army down on their heads if they don't,' Mickey said. 'You got to threaten these people, it's all they understand – carrot and stick.'

'Yes Hudson, make sure they get the full picture,' said Kathy.

Claire's annoyance at her friend was clear to Jonathan, who was standing beside her. 'Stop encouraging him. It's his stupid fault we're in this predicament,' she hissed. 'The less he offers an opinion and dictates what we're to do, the better off we'll be. I mean it, Kathy. Pull yourself together and listen to the rest of us instead of that idiot. This isn't a time to flirt with last night's shag!'

Kathy glared back, angry at first, but she pursed her lips, nodded and looked down to the ground.

'They say it is up to their chief, only he can decide after they have discussed all the problems with him,' Hudson translated, after a short discussion with the poachers. 'It is their way. They will have a meeting and the elders will sit and think about all the implications, and then the chief will announce the decision. This will be a very important matter for them, I think.'

'It's a bloody sight more important matter for us, mate.'

Claire said, 'Where is the village, Hudson? How much further is there to go?'

'They say it is not far – after the hills.'

Jonathan tried to see ahead, but the slopes of the Lebombo Mountains blocked the view. They were actually hills, not high mountains, maybe one-fifty to two hundred metres, he reckoned, but it was going to be hot and unpleasant walking through them. There was no wind and the temperature was already building in the valleys, even though it was winter. The sun penetrated shirts and baked the skin.

Jonathan's lips were parched. 'I'm not sure how much water we have left between us, because the poachers drank some of it at the kill. I think it would be best if we all stop talking and keep our mouths closed to preserve what moisture we have. We don't know when we'll drink again.'

11

A few dilapidated huts of mud and scraggy thatch blending into the bush, the village formed a focal point for several winding paths and a single vehicle track which found its way up the slope from the dry river crossing.

Nearby and unseen, a herd of goats nibbled at thin matter from which only they could gain any form of sustenance. Every now and again shrill human voices called out, interrupting the chirps of a few small birds; now and then, somewhere in the distance, a cow moaned.

The ground about the kraal was hard and swept, giving a clean, tidy appearance in spite of the ramshackle nature of the dwellings. In the shade of one hut, two women, their heads wrapped in scarves, pounded maize kernels in a giant mortar. A baby lay asleep beside one of them, and a third, in her late teens, suckled her infant as she listened to the gossip.

Sheltering from the sun under a large acacia to one side of the kraal, a group of three ageing men sat drinking sorghum beer and deliberating the problems and misfortunes which influenced their community. There were plenty of subjects to discuss, many of them for the umpteenth time, but whatever solutions the elders reached would be subject to the politics and banditry of the country.

'We have to decide what to do about the stock of maize and ground nuts which are hidden in the false grave, the one guarded on both sides by our fathers and their fathers before them,' said one.

'Yes, the thieves left us so little after their last raid. Soon it will run out, and we will have to break into our secret supply.'

'How can we do this without these men knowing we have more maize hidden?' said another.

'They will come back. It is as certain as the day follows the night. They always do. If it is not our village, then it is another. They roam freely, and the army, FRELIMO, does not protect us.'

'It was FRELIMO who stole from us the time before.'

There was supposed to be peace now, but not much had changed for these unfortunate peasants. If the army attacked them one time, the next it would be RENAMO, anti-government rebels, a few groups of which had refused to disband after the civil war; or maybe it would be unnamed bandits. Whatever they called themselves, they all stole the food, beat up the men, or sometimes killed them if they resisted or tried to interfere when the women were raped.

A scrawny cur sprawled in the sun near the women, its ribs as distinct as the fingers of a drumming hand as it panted away the rising temperature; why didn't it move into the shade? For no reason apparent to a human, it raised its head, a growl starting in its throat. Getting to its feet, it erupted into a high-pitched, irritating bark and bounded to the perimeter of the huts, facing something as yet unseen in the surrounding bush.

The women glanced at each other in alarm. In these troubled times no one ignored the warnings of dogs. The elders clambered to their feet. The youngest walked to where he might see what troubled the animals, for within seconds several others had joined the first in a strident chorus. It was his relieved shout which brought the people together to gawk at the strange procession trooping into the kraal, weary and nervous.

Jonathan stared back at the drawn and serious faces which confronted them. They were fascinated by Gudrun. He guessed they had never seen a woman as tall as her before, nor one with such pale hair.

What struck him was how skinny they all were, even the children. André's words about forgiving them poaching the odd animal for food assumed greater meaning.

The dogs kept up their yapping at the strangers until someone threw a stone and they scampered away to growl unhappily from a distance.

The poachers, still waving their assault rifles around with a complete lack of concern for safety, shoved the group into an empty round hut, accompanied by unintelligible shouting. Why were they being treated with such hostility? They were innocent witnesses to a crime which would never see a court. A glance around the group revealed a range of reactions from anger and rebellion to mute submission. The cold-blooded, medieval hacking of their colleague was stamped into every mind. The uncertainty of their future preyed on them.

Their captors had already said they wanted hostages, but that had been for protection from the rangers. Now it would be for money – but was there another cause, this time unknown? Without the killing, the thought of death would have been more remote; *it will not happen to me*. But the murder would not allow that illusion. The danger had become personal.

Although they were strangers to each other and aliens in

this land, there was no question that they had to unite to survive. But Jonathan's concern was that Mickey might rebel if he took a leading role. Mickey probably understood, but found it difficult to succumb to the collective need. *Every one of us is scared, and the fear is gnawing at our innards like a cancer. We all know the slightest wrong move – it might be anything – could trigger another violent reaction from these men.*

No one spoke. It was too soon to indulge in the futility of speculation.

The rickety door was dragged shut behind them. When his eyes had adjusted to the dim interior and he could see the hut was bare, Jonathan took Gudrun's hand and sat with his back to the wall. 'They've left the horns with you. That's odd.'

'They think we can't escape, so why should they worry? They will come and try to take them later, though.'

'Yes, and then what are you going to do?'

'I told you, they will not have these horns.'

Serious trouble loomed with Gudrun's attitude, but Jonathan wasn't prepared to argue about it, not now.

The others had also sat, leaving only Mickey Rider pacing about.

Jonathan examined their prison. The temperature was a little cooler than the exterior, which he estimated was in the high twenties, but the sun baked the earth outside, and hot air rose to enter the hut through the gap between the wall and the thatched roof. With the door closed and the humans inside, the heat began to build. The place stank. Smoke from years of cooking fires, boiled meat and the stale odours of prolonged human habitation had saturated the thatch and thickened the air. The door frame was dark with layers of grime from hosts of sweaty fingers.

The rondavel had been constructed from upright sticks rammed into the ground, the space between them packed with a mud and straw mixture. Jonathan kicked at the back wall, and a few lumps of the crumbling fill tumbled out, exposing the wood supports. He did it again and dug at the rest with his hands.

'Does anyone have a knife? If we can cut some of this wood away, it'll be easy to make a hole here.'

'Mine is in my pack,' Armand said. 'They 'ave it.'

'I've got one, let me get at it.' Mickey pushed forward.

'I thought *you* might.' Jonathan stepped back to allow Mickey access.

'What's that supposed to mean?'

'Please *mes amis*, we are all together in this. Stop the arguing, please,' Armand pleaded.

Jonathan nodded. He was stupid to goad the man. He went to see what he could through the gaps in the door. It had been fastened closed with wire twisted round nails on the outside. He said so, and Rider gave up trying to cut through the wood. He came over to see. 'A good kick will sort that out.'

'Better wait until we've a chance to escape unnoticed.'

'Better not be too long,' Rider said. 'You'll have us all waiting until they take us out and shoot us. We need to move quickly.'

Armand rose from his cross-legged position in one easy movement and walked over to the door to look at the fastening. 'We should wait a little to see what is 'appening. If we try to escape they may shoot us, but they may relax a little later.'

Hudson was barely visible in the gloom. 'Tonight they will celebrate, they will drink beer and eat meat. They will be happy and more relaxed. We should wait until it is dark anyway.'

Rider gave a resentful grunt and continued pacing. Armand returned to sit by Annette, putting his right hand down on the floor to take his weight. 'Aargh! *Merde!*'

'*Chéri?*'

Armand leapt to his feet, gasping something in French. He held up his hand. '*Merde,*' he swore again. 'Something stung me. My God it 'urts!'

Annette had her hand up to her mouth in horror, struggling to issue words that would not come. Mickey strode over, searched around and stamped hard on the floor. 'Scorpion. Dead now, not to worry.'

'No, Armand is allergic! He needs 'is injection. This is terrible.'

'What are you talking about?'

'Armand must have his auto injector, his EpiPen, to administer the adrenalin, or he is in great danger. *Armand, Chéri*, be brave, maybe it will not happen.' She clutched his upper arm in both her hands.

'What won't happen?' Gudrun said.

Claire and Kathy came over to the couple. 'Anaphylaxis?' Kathy said. 'We're cabin attendants, we're trained in first aid.'

'*Oui*, yes. It is serious. This needs more than first aid. He must have adrenalin.'

Armand was holding his right hand in his left and rocking back and forth. The hand was swelling rapidly. Already, after a couple of minutes, his breathing was becoming short and noisy.

'Surely you carry some with you?' said Jonathan.

'Yes, of course, but in his backpack. *They* 'ave it,' Annette yelled, jabbing her finger towards the door.

Hudson shouted something through the cracks in the door. Mickey joined him, bellowing. Gudrun screamed, 'Help!'

The two girls knelt beside Armand. Claire had her hand on his wrist. 'His pulse is racing. They must bring the pack here. Now!'

At the door, the others renewed their shouting, but still there was no response from the villagers.

Armand slumped into a foetal position, clutching his stomach.

'What can we do, Annette?' Jonathan was feeling helpless. But Annette wasn't paying attention to anything other than her husband.

As Armand's breathing became even more laboured, Kathy stood up. 'He's in anaphylactic shock. His throat is swelling up, making it difficult for him to breathe. It looks like he has stomach cramps, and his blood pressure will have dropped. His heart is racing to compensate.' She stretched up to whisper in Jonathan's ear. 'Without adrenalin, he might die because he cannot breathe, or he might have a cardiac arrest. This is extremely serious.'

Jonathan moved towards the entrance, changed his mind and gave Mickey the chance to do something. 'Can you kick the door out? They must return the backpack.'

'Stand back,' Rider ordered, and gave the thing a hefty boot. The wood cracked, and the wire stretched, but it didn't break. He tried again. The door sprung open. They burst out into dazzling, painful sunlight to face two assault rifles and two angry faces.

Hudson raised his open palms and gabbled at them. One of the men shouted at some others. More villagers gathered round. There was no sense of urgency, though, no one running to find the backpack.

'What can we do? I can't think. What are they doing, Hudson?' Gudrun clutched his arm. 'Armand could die there without his injection.'

Hudson listened to the chatter for a moment. 'I think they've emptied out the packs, but they don't know what they're looking for. They don't understand the urgency.'

Mickey thrust his head forward. 'Well bloody tell them.'

Taking it in turns, Jonathan and Mickey had been cutting and breaking the dry wood in the back wall of the hut. Using one of the broken sticks, Jonathan was working to enlarge the hole in the mud-and-straw fill.

Mickey was on his knees. He sat back and pointed at the opening. 'It's still not bloody big enough. Hudson's got to get through. Here, gimme that, I'll do it quicker than you.'

'It's all right, I'll do it for now.'

Mickey's hand covered Jonathan's and crushed it, forcing him to drop the stick. Mickey picked it up and shoved Jonathan aside. He didn't speak, but his look said it all. *'Just try it, just fucking try it.'*

Jonathan didn't. Instead he argued, 'If we make it bigger now, they'll see it. We need to stop and start again after dark.'

'I'm telling you, we need to get out of here right now. They'll kill us before tonight.'

'Why would they do that after all the trouble of getting us here? And what about Armand? We can't leave him here to die; and Annette, what about her?'

'Your bloody dithering will get us killed. You've got to take your chances when you can.'

'Mickey, you and I don't see eye to eye, that's a fact. Let's accept it for now and sort out our differences after we're out of here. Right now we have to work together to save us all, and that includes the weakest ones, Armand and Annette at the moment. Please.'

'Right, so why should I listen to you, not you listen to me who's got more experience?'

Hudson squatted next to them. 'Mickey, Jonathan, please hear me. You have to stop your fighting, to save us all. I'm sorry Mickey but Jonathan is right. The best chance for us to get out will be tonight, not now. We must wait until they are drunk and the darkness can cover us. If we leave in the light, they will track us down very quickly.'

Jonathan sat with his back covering the hole and looked

across at Mickey. *Why will he only listen to Hudson without arguing?* He drew Gudrun closer to him and linked his forefinger through hers; it was too hot for closer contact.

Mickey and Hudson were also sitting with their backs to the wall. Both had their eyes closed in response to the soporific atmosphere. Opposite them were Kathy, Claire and Annette. Armand was on his side, facing the wall with his head resting on Annette's thigh. Jonathan watched his shoulders heaving and his knees drawing up on every inhalation with the effort of trying to pull air into his lungs. He was unable to shut out the rasp that came with the man's every agonised breath.

Annette dabbed at moisture on her husband's face, stroked his damp hair and murmured inaudible soothing words.

'Where do her tears come from?' Gudrun said. 'We're all so thirsty there's surely no fluid left in any of us.'

Jonathan shrugged. All thoughts of rescue, even of what would become of them, were pushed into the background in trying to cope with the here and now: clothing which dragged across his sticky skin, the stifling lack of air movement, a parched mouth and Armand's painful struggle to breathe.

His voice hoarse, Jonathan said, 'Hudson, please ask them again for water. They took ours, and we've had nothing to drink for hours.'

Hudson clambered to his feet. 'I can try, but they don't care about us.'

'They'll bloody care if one of us dies in their hands,' Mickey grumbled.

Hudson went to the door and shouted through the cracks. There was a lengthy reply from somewhere outside; it sounded far away. Hudson turned back to the room. 'They are already fetching water, they say. I think it is some distance. They also said they cannot find the EpiPen. Maybe it fell out of the pack when they took our water, or maybe a child took it to play with.'

A cry of despair from Annette was suppressed into a whimper.

Kathy came over to Gudrun and whispered, 'This is terrible. I don't see how he will recover.'

There was movement outside the door. It was yanked open. Harsh light flooded the room. Jungly was there, cautious, his AK47 pushing ahead of him as he stepped into the hut. A woman filled the doorway. She lowered what looked like a twenty-litre paraffin can from off her head so she could get through. Laying it down on the floor with a wary look at the foreigners, she retreated outside. Hudson asked Jungly something. The villager called to the woman, who gave a short answer.

Mickey got to his feet, his focus on the can, but Jungly threatened him back to the wall with his rifle. 'What's the matter, you bloody savage? That's for us isn't it?'

'The woman has gone to find a cup so we can share the water without spilling it,' Hudson explained. 'He wants you to wait.'

'Huh.'

Jungly stood in the doorway, his AK tracking the room from one person to the next. Jonathan said out loud, 'These guys worry me. This one, he's so nervous, he's fidgeting, and his fingers are playing around the trigger of that thing. One little fright or slip and it'll go off.'

No one answered him.

'I think Armand's breathing is getting shorter,' Jonathan said to Gudrun.

An old tin can arrived to serve as a mug. Jungly took it from the woman and tossed it to Mickey, before hastening out of the hut and rewiring the door. To his credit, instead of helping himself, Mickey filled the tin and took it to Annette.

Armand was not able to drink, but she moistened his lips before drinking it herself. One by one, Mickey dispensed tins of water to them all. Jonathan grimaced at the foul taste, but none of them complained – it was water. They had three tins each, downed swiftly.

Jonathan said, 'We'd better stop there for a while, we don't know when they'll give us more.'

No one disagreed; in fact there was complete silence. Jonathan gave Gudrun a questioning glance, putting a finger to his ear. On the other side of the hut, Annette was trembling. Armand was still at last, his agony over.

<h1 style="text-align:center">12</h1>

The streaks of light from the door lost their intensity. Darkness fell swiftly when it began, and with it a gradual fall in temperature. Outside, movement in the village was increasing. A fire had been lit in the central area between the huts, and sounds of simple music with a persistent beat drifted into the room.

'We can only escape after they've been drinking a while and they're happy celebrating,' Jonathan said. 'Is the beer powerful stuff, Hudson?'

'It may be. They brew it in the village, and it can be very strong. Sometimes it is even poisonous!'

Jonathan beckoned to Claire and Kathy, who were on the other side of the room. Keeping his voice down, he said, 'We will have to leave Armand's body here. It's going to be terrible for Annette. Can you persuade her it's the best thing, the only way we can escape?'

'We can try. God. Poor woman.'

Mickey said, 'We'll have to force her if she won't agree. We can't leave her here alone with these savages.'

'All right. We'll keep a good watch on the party and wait

for the best time to leave. Mickey, you're the strongest, can you rip out the rest of that hole so we can get through when we think it's safe? If we try to leave through the door, we risk being seen.'

Mickey knelt at the hole. 'I'm ahead of you. Already there.' He held up the stick to prove it.

Jonathan pulled Hudson to one side. 'Will you relay my instructions to Mickey, please? He accepts you, but gets angry when I take the lead.'

'A good plan, Jonathan. I'll do it.'

'First thing is to ask him to lead the group out of the hole and gather everyone together about twenty metres into the bush. We'll move on from there.'

'I'll do it.'

Jonathan suggested a plan to the others. 'Here's what I think we should do: you three ladies will have to handle Annette, all right? Gudrun is the strongest of you if you need to force her. I'll bring the water. Hudson, please be prepared to talk us out of any difficult situations. Mickey's going to get the hole open wide enough. Hudson, I think you should please wait by the door to talk to the guard while the others escape. I'll go last, after you. I'll push the water can through, you wait on the outside and take it from me. Is everyone happy with that, or have a better idea?'

None of the others disagreed.

'I think it's important we stay in a tight group, no one gets left behind, and no one talks or makes a sound until we're well clear. Once we get moving, if anyone needs to stop, we all stop. Okay?'

Mumblings of agreement.

Gudrun asked, 'Which direction are we going to go?'

'Good point. The first thing will be to get as far from the village as we can, then we can try to get oriented. When we last looked through the door, there was some thin cloud cover, so we probably won't be able to pick up the Southern Cross. If we can see the outline of the Lebombo Mountains, then we head that way. If we can't, maybe the point where the moon rises will give us a rough idea of east. We want to go west.'

More murmurs of understanding. Mickey must have agreed, because he didn't argue or try to assert his leadership, but he did ask, 'What about lions? What are we going to do if we bump into them?'

In the darkness, only vague outlines could be seen. Facial expressions were invisible, but they were all waiting for Jonathan to provide an answer. By making a few sensible suggestions he had taken control, had become the leader of this disparate group, as far out of their depth as they could be.

'I haven't got a clue, Mickey. Remember, though, André told us the poachers go into the park to get their meat, because this part of Mozambique is so devoid of game. It's all been killed. There's no food for lions, so there's not much chance of meeting one until after we go through the fence.'

Whether his theory was true or not, they were relieved. It was one worry they could put behind them for a while.

'I'll carry the water, but in case it spills or I drop it, I think we should drink as much as we can before we leave, don't you?'

Again there was no challenge. As the time for escape and more danger approached, everyone's nerves were stretched. It was not surprising they quickly accepted plans founded on common sense.

Claire spoke gently to Annette while Kathy held the French-woman's hand in both of hers. Annette shook her head violently when she realised what was being said. '*Non! Non!* I will not leave my Armand. He is my life. I understand you need to go, but I will stay with Armand.'

'But—'

'*Non!* Is final, I am staying 'ere, I will take my chance, but I will not leave my 'usband. I will not.'

The three men maintained a constant uncomfortable watch by taking it in turns to stoop and peer through the cracks in the low door. After two hours, the village party was in full swing. Simple repetitive tunes were accompanied by enthusiastic drumming. The women sang, ululated and danced, accompanied by laughter and drunken shouting from the spectators. In the hut, the only illumination was a faint orange flicker which found its way through the door from the fire outside. After watching the dancing for a while, Jonathan could see nothing in the hut until his eyes adjusted.

'I reckon it's time to go,' Mickey said. 'I'm going to open that hole.'

'Is the guard still outside?'

'Nah, I think he's gone to join in the piss-up.'

'Let's do it, we can't wait forever. Claire, Kathy, it's time.' Jonathan inclined his head in the direction of Annette, not that they would be able see him.

Mickey was still looking through the door. 'Shit! Hang on, there's something going on.'

The sound of an approaching diesel vehicle penetrated the hut. Headlights swung across the entrance, sending brief slivers of light round the room before being switched off.

Jonathan joined Mickey and peered through an adjacent crack. Two strangers were walking towards the celebrations. They joined some older men from the community on the far side of the fire, the glow from which lent an orange tint to every individual. Their clothing was neat and smart compared to the grubby and tatty garments of the locals. One of them, a black man, was running to fat, unlike any of the villagers, while the other was short and wiry and appeared to be of mixed race. His skin was darker than a European's but much paler than the locals, and his features were almost oriental. The group were looking at two other men who were digging up the ground. One plucked a rhino horn from the hole and handed it up to his elder. The other digger held another horn out for inspection.

Mickey swore. 'They've got a cache of horns there, the bastards!'

Jonathan stood upright to ease his back. 'Those men must be buyers,'

'They'll be coming to get these ones at any moment. We'd better move.'

A long and horrified scream pierced the celebrations. The music stopped. The drums faltered and died. As one, the villagers turned to see what was going on. An ugly rattle of gunfire shattered the party atmosphere. Flames licked up the roof of a hut on the far side of the settlement. Women screamed, men shouted. People were running, scattering into the night.

'Christ!' Mickey said. 'They're under attack. We've got to get out of here, fast.'

'Agreed.' Jonathan turned from watching the action. 'They're burning the huts. Come on, let's go. Mickey, get the hole open. Girls, get Annette out. No argument, we'll be burned alive or shot if we stay.'

'Fuck! I can't get this bloody stick to budge,' yelled Mickey. 'It's too thick. We'll have to take the door.'

Jonathan had already kicked the door once. It held fast. He tried again. Mickey pushed him out of the way and booted it hard. The fastening gave, the single hinge broke and the door fell outwards.

Annette was clinging to her man. 'No, no. I will not leave Armand.'

Claire had her round the waist, and Kathy had her arm,

but they were trying to pull two bodies. Her grip on Armand's wrist had the strength of panic, and her beloved dead husband was being dragged across the floor. They stopped. Gudrun stepped in and prised Annette's fingers apart. The other two half-carried, half-shoved the poor woman outside. Gudrun picked up the sack, tucked it under her arm as best she could and followed them.

With the others ahead of him, Jonathan checked to see if anyone had noticed them. The strangers were running for their car. The fat one was climbing in, but the small man stopped. He had seen movement. It must have been Gudrun, for he stared after her until she disappeared into the trees. His attention returned to the hut where Jonathan stood at the door, holding the can of water. The two men remained still, staring at each other.

The exchange of looks was significant. There was something important in it, something which bound two complete strangers together in an indecipherable manner. It lasted for a very long ten seconds, before the man disappeared into the darkness, and Jonathan followed his group.

A backdrop of intense gunfire lasted for a short while, before dwindling to sporadic shots. It urged them to hurry, to get well clear before making any decisions about anything.

The ground was flat and the going should have been easy, but there was no moon. Jonathan, in the lead, kept up as fast a pace as he could, but it was still slow. Trees materialised out of the darkness a few steps ahead, and he would have to divert around them. Thin branches scratched his face, and several times he almost tripped on unseen hazards. Subdued grumblings came from those behind, who were going through the same experience. To maintain a constant direction while twisting and turning around these obstacles was only possible if they kept the burning village at their backs, but when the fires died it would have to be intelligent guesswork, and far from certain. They would need to identify west before then. He had read of men going round in a big circle in deserts or forests when they had nothing to aim at.

He stopped and everyone closed up behind him. He was carrying the water by the can's wire handle, and some ten kilos were digging into his hand. They had put enough distance between them and the village to take a break. They were all hungry, and some were feeling weak.

'Are you all okay? Annette?'

She did not answer him, Kathy did. 'She's doing okay. I think she's accepted the situation. She's moving willingly, but like a zombie.'

'We'll look after her,' Claire said. 'Keep going, don't worry.'

Jonathan felt for Gudrun's hand and for the first time noticed the sack. He pulled her to one side and whispered so the others couldn't hear. 'What the hell are you doing with that? You're crazy!' Her penetrating look challenged him. They were about to have their first serious argument.

'This must be returned to the park, it is not theirs.' She tossed her head in the direction of the village.

'It's the horns those people want, not us. Bringing them with you is putting everyone in danger, they'll kill for them. You've no right to jeopardise other people's lives like this.'

'The poachers are most likely dead now in that raid, you heard the shooting. And the bandits or whatever they are don't even know about us.'

'I wouldn't bet on it. That stranger watched us leave, I saw him. I can't believe you were so daft as to bring it.'

'Jonathan, don't tell me what to do! These people will not have this horn, understand that. They will *not* have it. I made a decision, I'm carrying it, and that is that.' She turned away and went back to the group.

The anger in her reply stunned him. Until this crisis, Jonathan had not seen Gudrun get angry, and it had never been with him, but the stress of the situation was obviously taking its toll.

Hunger had nothing to do with the sudden cavity inside him. They had never disagreed about anything before, and he had never considered the possibility they would. Did she feel the same for him as he did for her? He loved her so much, but that didn't mean he wasn't cross with her. Now was not the time for a fight, though.

Back to the immediate problem. 'Does anyone know what time the moon will rise?'

Kathy had been the only one up in the night. 'It was there, low down, before three last night, I went to the loo about then.'

Unseen, Claire coughed.

Jonathan thought for a few seconds. 'We're in the southern hemisphere, and it's winter, so it should rise north of east, but I've never taken note. How does everyone feel? I think we should wait here for the moon, and we can see something. We could be heading parallel to the hills, or even further away from them. This slow pace is not achieving much except making us tired. It'll be about four hours.'

'Some of those buggers might be after us, and we're sitting ducks staying here,' Mickey said.

'I know, but can they track us in the pitch black? Once the moon's up we'll be able to move faster, but without knowing which way to go, we could be making it easier for them to catch up with us when it's light enough.'

'Huh. Best get some kip then.' Mickey brushed the dirt around him and stretched out.

A few heads indicated silent agreement in the dark and followed his example. But the temperature had fallen, and it wouldn't be easy sleeping on the cold ground.

Hudson had no difficulty, though, and soon snored. Gudrun, who was closest, shoved him awake. 'Shh!'

'Sorry.'

Mickey too snored, stopped, and started again.

'Shh!' someone hissed. It must have been Kathy; she was next to him. He grunted and went back to sleep. Jonathan slept a little, but kept waking and checking the time. He was tired, footsore, hungry, thirsty, didn't know where the hell they were and, having taken control of the group, knew they counted on him to get them out of this. *Mickey is tough and presents no physical problem. Claire and Kathy are doing all right. They've adopted a professional approach and caring for Annette will keep their thoughts off their own miseries. Annette herself is our weakest link. She's moving mechanically, a clockwork automaton following her capable guides.*

Provided the two girls can keep her and themselves going, we should make it to the border. Or can we? Hudson is difficult to read. He's a different ethnic group, and his expressions are not the same as the rest of us. What discomfort does he hide? He's wheezed and panted his way through the night loudly enough to make me wonder if he's going to have a heart attack. We're going to find it bloody difficult to move his bulk if he goes down. Gudrun, on the other hand, is no problem, she's physically tough and so damned determined she'll outlast the lot of us.

So, on and off, they slept. Jonathan woke instantly when Gudrun shook him. 'The moon's coming up, behind the cloud over there.'

Hudson squinted at his watch. 'It is half past two – a bit more.'

Jonathan had had the foresight to chuck the tin they'd used for drinking into the can. Each gulped the water, while others fidgeted for their turn with the makeshift mug. He said, 'There are no stars – can anyone see the outline of the hills?'

No one answered him.

Jonathan shrugged. 'The moon's just risen, let's keep it behind our right shoulders for the moment. That'll keep us heading roughly west, but we'll have to correct as it travels over the sky to the north of us. Mickey, would you like to lead? I'll stay at the back and try to keep us going in the same direction until we can see the mountains.'

'Right. It's the only way to do it.' Mickey sounded resentful.

Annette was shivering, so Claire put her arm around her as the group fell into line and prepared to move. Hudson was standing with Jonathan, looking back in the direction they had come. 'The fire in the village is out now,' he said. 'I pray no one is following us.'

13

Hlulani and Kuhlula moved faster than most could in the dark. Keeping together and clutching their guns, they had escaped from the raiders who were after the stock of rhino horn and what grain was hidden in the village. The young poachers had run for their lives, deep into the bush.

Hlulani scratched his thick, matted hair. 'We're on our own now, you and me. We must get the horns the tall woman carried. They are ours, we took the risks to get them. It will mean a lot of money for us. We can share it between the two of us instead of the whole village.'

The other lad rubbed his sore and itchy eyes. 'I don't understand why the old man wanted to leave it with her. It would have been better to sell it with the others.'

'He said if she had it, it would keep her quiet and avoid a fight with her, maybe someone would be killed. He said we were already in enough trouble and there would be much more if we hurt another one. He said it was safe and we could get it later. Huh!'

'You think she left it in the hut? I'm scared to go back with those men searching the place, Hlulani. Anyway, they will have found the horn by the time we get back.'

'I'm older than you, I make the decisions. We've got to try. We'll be careful, don't worry. You keep a lookout, I'll search the hut.'

They returned to their village and, with Kuhlula watching from the darkness of the trees, Hlulani crept round to the hut door. The thieves were digging up the trove on the other side of the village. What thatched roofs that had been torched were now smouldering remains, which were still glowing and providing some dim light, little of which found its way into the hut.

For some reason, like the ones on either side of it, the place had not been set alight. Hlulani saw nothing but the odd pale shape, so felt around with his feet. Something soft; he knelt and touched the leg of a body. He was used to death, it did not bother him. He carried on feeling his way around, but the rest of the hut floor was bare.

Back outside, he said to Kuhlula, 'The foreigners have taken the horn with them. We must track them and get it back. They will be weak and slow, and we can catch them as soon as we have a moon.'

Together they cast around at the back of the hut to find whatever signs the group had left. It was too dark to follow the spoor with any speed, even though the seven had left an easy trail. But when the moon rose and the light improved around three o'clock, Hlulani and Kuhlula were able to speed up. Sometimes they even broke into an easy run they could keep up for hours, provided they could see the trail.

'Why is it taking us so long to reach the border? It only took a couple of hours to get to the village when the poachers were pushing us.'

Jonathan was glad to exchange a few words to take his mind off what was going to be a difficult conflict with

Gudrun as well as his exposed position. Being at the back of the line made him nervous, and he kept looking behind searching for danger. 'We don't know the quickest way, Kathy,' he said. 'We may be going at an angle to the fence instead of straight towards it. We've no way of telling.'

Although it was night-time, the blanket of cloud, thin though it was, had retained a little of the day's heat. The exercise, coupled with the tension, was warming. Jonathan's skin was damp from a light sweat, sticky with salt and gritty with dust. His scratches stung when he wiped his forehead. Maintaining direction was his primary concern, but he was also worried about the others.

Annette and Hudson must be exhausted. There's no option but to continue, though. If anyone's chasing us, they'll know we're heading for the fence and will try to ambush us there. To do that they have to get ahead of us, so we've got to keep moving. If only Gudrun hadn't been so stupid and selfish in bringing the horn ... It defies common sense.

At times, Jonathan fantasised on what his first meal was going to be, but water was more important than food. He was a little light-headed. Everyone else must surely feel the same, and in that weakened state fear came easily. A threat of some kind lurked in each of their minds, waiting to strike. He overheard Kathy whispering to her friend, 'I'm scared as hell, Claire.'

'So am I, we all are. We must focus on Annette, that's our duty, and it'll take our minds off fear.'

'You're so bloody sensible, but then you always are. Thanks, I'll try.'

Jonathan argued that they should not finish the water unless they had to and, moan about that as much as they did, no one disagreed.

'Having to stop so often is slowing us down,' Gudrun said at one rest.

'I know, and it worries me. Mickey, too. He grunts his frustration every time we take a break, but we have to stick with the slowest.'

Hudson defied Jonathan's earlier doubts. He did not seem to be any more tired than when they started. He made noisy progress, but remained strong. Annette, though, was plodding along in a trance, dragging her feet, thoroughly demoralised and incapable of contributing to the group in any way.

Claire and Kathy supported her all the time – not physically, but in whispers. One of them stayed in front of her, the other close behind, and every now and again they changed over.

'Let me help you with Annette,' Gudrun offered as she sat next to Claire at one stop, laying the sack on the ground between them.

'No, it's okay, thanks. She knows and trusts us as we've been close ever since Armand …'

'Do you believe in first impressions?'

'Mine are mostly right. Strange topic for the moment, though. Why?'

'I always follow them. I clicked with Jonathan straightaway, and it's been wonderful. I think you and I could be good friends.'

Claire's teeth glinted in the darkness. 'My first impression of you was the same.' She held her hand out. Gudrun took it and lingered in the grip for a few seconds.

'God, my hair feels disgusting, it's filthy and messy. You're so lucky – no, you're clever having a pixie cut. I'm going to get one when we get back.'

'You're crazy, you're hair is gorgeous long and braided. Please don't cut it, it suits you so well.'

'You're too kind, Claire. I know it looks good, but it takes so much work compared to yours. And now, in this situation, it's just annoying.'

'You're not going to be in this situation much longer.'

'I bloody hope so.'

Annette leapt up, catching their attention. She said something in French, something about Armand. Suddenly she ran off, back the way they had come, crying, 'Armand, Armand!'

Claire sprang to her feet. Gudrun was quicker. She sprinted into the darkness, her long strides gaining ground. But she tripped on something and fell into the dust. Claire dashed past her. 'Where is she? Annette, Annette, stop please.'

Gudrun was on her feet again.

Jonathan reached her. 'What's going on?'

'Annette,' was all she said and ran off after Claire. 'Where did she go?'

'I don't know. Oh God, this is awful. We have to find her, we cannot leave her.'

There was a cry of pain from ahead of them. Together, they raced towards it. Annette was on all fours under a small tree nursing her head.

'What's the matter, dear? What's up?' Kathy had caught up with them.

'It's her face.' Claire was peering at the flow of blood running from the woman's forehead and her dirt-smudged cheeks. 'She must have run into a branch.'

Jonathan said, 'Girls, is she all right? Time is passing, we must move.'

Gudrun squatted and, putting her hands under Annette's arms, lifted her to her feet. Annette's will had gone; her legs were jelly, and almost collapsed beneath her. But the Icelander held her up and let her cry herself out with her head on Gudrun's shoulder. Gently, she turned Annette around and, holding her arm, supported her back to the group.

'We should rest a little bit longer for Annette's sake, Jonathan. And I think we should have some more water after that chase.'

'Here.' Jonathan passed the almost empty can. 'Go easy, there's not much left.'

Gudrun felt around where she had been sitting. 'The horns, they've gone. Where's my sack? I left it here, where is it? Hudson, did you move it?'

A deep, patient reply. 'No, Gudrun, it was not me.'

'I've got it here, darling. Relax, it's quite safe. It must be getting heavy, though – I'll carry it for you, if you like.' The voice was sneering, teasing.

'I *don't* like. Give it back to me, Mickey. The horns are mine until I hand them over to the parks people.'

'Suit yourself. Just trying to help.' He handed the sack up to her.

Still in front of him, she made a point of checking the contents before sitting beside Jonathan. 'Bloody man,' she hissed. 'What does he think he's doing taking my horns; testing me, perhaps? You think he wanted to steal them?'

'Maybe he wants to get rid of them, so we can be safe.'

Gudrun gave a derisive snort.

'Well done.' Jonathan meant her getting the horns back, but added, 'Are you okay after your fall? Is Annette badly hurt?'

'I'm good. Poor Annette has a big scratch. It's hard to tell in this light, but I don't think it's as bad as it looks. Head wounds bleed a lot.'

Jonathan retired into his own troubled mind. Gudrun appeared to have put their brief argument behind her already, but he couldn't. For him, issues had to be solved before they were forgotten. *She assumes she's right in bringing those horns, but she's put every one of us at risk. I've got to persuade her that her attitude will be damaging to our future – we can't take clients on without being responsible for their safety.*

Because she's so determined, this has the potential to be a big divide between us, and I'm dreading it. Will this split us apart? Please, no. I don't want to argue with her, ever. We're going to have to talk this out, but not now, not while we're so stressed. We have to reach safety first – then I'll tackle it.

He wanted to hold her, but his troubled mind wouldn't let him make the move.

Gudrun did, though. She ran a gentle hand over his coarse two-day-old stubble. 'You need a shower, you stink.'

How does she always manage to put me at ease, to push any desire for argument into the background? He had to grin at her. 'So, my beautiful woman, do you.' He stood and extended a hand to her. 'Come, we need to keep going.'

Not long afterwards, Mickey remarked how dark it was to the right of them.

'Maybe it's the mountains.' Apart from answering Gudrun, it was the first time Hudson had said anything since they had grouped together outside the village.

'God! About time.'

'We need to change direction,' Jonathan said. 'We crossed the mountains at ninety degrees before, now we're going at an angle. We need to turn right a bit. We should be climbing soon, but they're not high. Where we came into Mozambique, there were only a couple of ridges to cross before the fence. If there are no problems we could reach it within an hour.'

A murmur of cautious optimism ran through the group. In an effort to keep morale up, Jonathan had been issuing platitudes every so often: "Can't be much further; Not long now; the hills aren't far away." He knew they had ceased to believe him, but now, with the physical presence of the dark mass ahead, there was renewed hope.

Step by step the gradient increased. Jonathan's position at

the back of the line allowed him to see how everyone was performing. Tired bodies hauled themselves up the slope; every step an effort. As they climbed, the sky to the east began to lighten. Details of the bush around them emerged from the twilight. They followed around the curve of the hill, keeping above the valley to their left where the vegetation was more dense. In the early light it was doubtful they would see the fence itself, but the track which ran beside it should have been obvious. Reaching the top of the first ridge, though, they saw no sign of it.

'One more ridge. I pray that is all,' Hudson said as they descended.

Once the sun had shown itself, it sprang from the horizon to dominate the earth and banish the cold night air. Air currents drifted upwards from the warming of the hilltops. They struggled up the second slope with the ghost of despair hovering above, ready to envelope each of them if the border was yet another ridge away.

But it was not. As they emerged from the bush with a view into the next valley, Mickey, still in the lead, shouted, 'It's there! The fence is there.'

14

Mentally, they tore down the slope. Physically, it was a lot slower, because they were too tired and too sore from the night's trek to put much energy into reaching it.

The fence was set in clear ground. In this area it consisted of several horizontal strands of cable stretched between the posts and backed with chain-link wire fencing, in all about six foot high. On the South African side lay the dirt track used by the army.

With no ability to cut a hole in the wire, they would need to find an existing gap made by poachers or refugees, or climb over it.

Jonathan was again the first to voice what they should do. 'I think the ladies should rest here in the shade. Remember, if they're following us, they'll aim to catch us here at the border, so we're not out of the woods yet. In fact this could be the most dangerous part of our escape, so be careful. I suggest Mickey and Hudson go to the left along the fence and look for a hole. I'll do the same to the right. Let's walk along the border for fifteen minutes, then come back and report. If we don't find anything we'll try to climb over.'

'Good idea,' said Gudrun, 'but I'll come with you. I don't think anyone should be alone in this place.'

Mickey grumbled his sour agreement.

Gudrun picked up her sack. It was obvious she wasn't going to leave the horns alone again. She joined Jonathan at the fence, which ran in a dead straight line until it disappeared over a rise. They walked at an easy pace, lacking the will to stride out. She was cheerful and optimistic, reflecting everyone else's mood. This awful experience was almost over, freedom was within reach. Jonathan agreed, of course, but the thorn of her recklessness still pricked him, and he needed to discuss it. He was quiet, thinking on how best to tackle the matter when the time was right but at the same time avoid an ugly confrontation which might threaten their relationship.

It was clear Gudrun saw no conflict between them. She again ran her fingers over his stubble. 'You're looking rough, like some hero in an action movie.'

He could not help but wilt with her affection. 'But twice as tired. You, on the other hand, are as stunning as always.'

She laughed. 'Liar!' Then, 'I wonder how often the army patrols the border – do you think it's every day?'

Jonathan took off his hat and wiped his forehead. 'I've no idea. I hope so. We must be here before them if they do, it's early still.'

'Time to turn back.'

Mickey and Hudson still moved in the opposite direction. Ten minutes had gone by and there were no signs anyone had been in the area at all. They stopped and listened for a moment, hoping they might hear a vehicle.

'Let's stretch it to the top of the rise and see what's on the other side.' It was best to put off the difficult discussion and leave it until that night when, with any luck, they would be refreshed and feeling close to normal again.

* * *

Kuhlula and Hlulani looked down to the border from the ridge above it. They could not see the white people but knew they were down there somewhere. They had to catch them before the fence, and were confident they could. They knew the tourists' energy levels were low from the short steps some were taking, and often the dirt was scuffed where weary feet had not been lifted clear of the ground.

They trotted down the hillside and into the bush at the valley bottom. It was not far to the fence from there, so the foreigners must be close. Hlulani reached the edge of the vegetation where it had been cut back short of the border. He stopped, scanned up and down the fence line and beckoned Kuhlula forward. About fifty metres from them were two tourists walking in the opposite direction.

The poachers retreated into the cover of the trees. Keeping low, they moved from one dense bush to the next in complete silence, peering round each one to make sure they were not seen as they gained on the foreigners, until they could re-enter the cleared area close behind them.

Jonathan and Gudrun reached the top of the rise. There was nothing showing any promise, so they turned back. Mickey and Hudson were already walking back towards them.

Jonathan raised both arms in an empty gesture. Hudson acknowledged.

'What the hell –?'

Mickey and Hudson were running towards them, shouting. It was impossible to hear. Both men were waving their arms as they ran.

'What on earth are they on about?'

'I don't know. Weird.'

A movement in the corner of his eye. He glanced round. A face topped by a mass of woolly hair was low down behind

Gudrun. An arm was reaching for the sack she was slinging from her right hand.

'Watch out—'

Jungly made a grab for the sack, trying to wrench it from her. But Gudrun had twisted the neck around her wrist, and it was never going to come free. She yanked back on the sack, lifting the little poacher off his feet, but he wouldn't let go.

Jonathan went for him, but an AK47 was pointing at his stomach. He stopped. Red Eyes was so nervous his weapon was shaking, as was the other rifle slung over his shoulder. Jonathan took a step towards him.

Gudrun had her own fight. She smashed her left fist into Jungly's face and wrenched back on the sack. It came free. Swinging it over her shoulder, she aimed at the scruffy head. Four kilos of horn connected with an audible thump, and the young poacher crumpled to the ground. In her rage she raised the sack again.

'Stop, you'll kill him!'

'My rhino will kill him.' Her words were venomous, but she lowered her arm. 'That would be some justice, at least.'

Jonathan saw that his boy was petrified, unable to meet his eyes. He stepped up to the muzzle of the assault rifle, gripped it and turned it aside. The lad's hold relaxed. Jonathan carefully removed the gun from his grasp. Red Eyes stared at Jonathan's outstretched other hand, uncomprehending at first, but followed the white man's look and handed over Jungly's weapon as well.

Mickey was almost there, with poor fat Hudson struggling along behind as he laboured his way up the slope to help. Mickey was out of breath, and Hudson was bent over with his hands on his knees, wheezing for air.

'Thanks Mickey, Hudson. A bit late, but thanks for trying.'

Mickey glared at Gudrun. 'If you hadn't brought that thing along, this wouldn't have happened, and I wouldn't feel so fucked right now.'

Jonathan let his feelings be known through a meaningful look at her. He wasn't going to show public support for Mickey. Gudrun made some remark under her breath and set off ahead of them to where the other women were waiting. They left the two poachers where they were. Jonathan caught up with her. 'Are you okay? I thought you would kill him.'

'I'm good. You were brave to challenge him with his gun.'

'He was never going to shoot. He hasn't got it in him.'

They told Claire and Kathy what had happened, and asked about Annette.

'Poor thing's in a world of her own, almost delirious. She's exhausted mentally and physically and needs rest, not to mention a doctor.'

'There are no breaks in the fence, so we'll have to climb over. Will she make it?'

'We'll get her over, somehow or other.'

Mickey had a thought. 'We should let off a few rounds from these AKs. That might attract the army patrols.'

'Brilliant idea.' Jonathan had never seen an AK47, other than in pictures. He examined it.

Mickey said, 'Here, give it to me. I know what I'm doing.' He pressed the catch and released the magazine, which had about six rounds in it. Looking the weapon over he said, 'This one's pretty manky, barrel's corroded. Don't want it blowing up in my face. Let's see the other.

'This one's better. They're old with these wood butts, both Type 3.' He checked the magazine for free movement of the rounds, then took the contents of the first one and put them in the second.

'Don't use them all at once, Mickey, we might need another chance, and there are wild animals on the other side.'

'Right.'

The volley shattered the early-morning peace. To the

15

They were never going to be friends, but it seemed they were no longer going to fight. It was mid-morning and Jonathan, Gudrun and Mickey were downing a fantastic first beer in the otherwise empty bar. Gudrun had not let anyone take the sack from her. In fact, none of the park's staff had questioned what it was. They must have thought it was some possessions she had managed to salvage. She was waiting to hand it over to the chief ranger and didn't want to arouse any comment before it became Parks Board property.

'I'm going to the toilet.' Gudrun pushed the sack in Jonathan's direction. 'Watch it, please.'

'Sure.' Jonathan stood and wandered over to the window.

Behind his back, Mickey grabbed the sack and dumped it over the bar. He grinned at the barman, put a finger to his lips and tucked a fifty-rand note into the man's shirt pocket. He joined Jonathan at the window.

'Pretty little bird, that.' Mickey pointed. 'Looks like a sparrow.'

'Does a bit. I don't know anything about local birds, except the big ones.' Jonathan turned back to his chair. The sack was gone. He looked all round the table, shoving the chairs to one side. 'Where's the sack? I only turned my back for a minute.'

'I dunno, mate. I saw Gudrun leave it with you, and that's the last I saw of it. Can't have got far.'

Jonathan took the three short strides to reach the bar. 'Have you got a sack there behind the counter?'

The barman swallowed and retreated under Jonathan's glare. 'No, sir.'

Jonathan glanced round the bar area. It would have been impossible for anyone to take the sack out of the room without him seeing, even from the window.

'I'm coming to look.'

'Sir, the bar is out of bounds to guests.'

'I'm coming to look.' He saw it as soon as he lifted the bar flap. He picked up the sack and glared at the barman.

The man licked his lips and shook his head. 'I don't know, sir. I didn't know it was here, sir.'

'How did it get here?'

The barman's hand was shaking. 'I … I don't know, sir.'

Jonathan took the sack back to the table. He glowered, but said nothing.

'I'm going out for a smoke.' Mickey walked away, pulling a cigarette packet from his shirt pocket.

Jonathan went back to the barman, who avoided eye contact. He reached forward and pulled the exposed banknote out of the man's pocket. 'Did that other chap give you this?'

Eyes down. Silence.

'All right, relax. I understand.' He slapped the note onto the counter and returned to his chair. *So much for loyalty gained from sharing danger, from working together to survive; so much for making the peace after all the tension.*

With the sack in a firm grip, Jonathan went outside to find Mickey. *Is this his idea of a joke? Was he hoping to take it and sell the horns?*

Rider was nowhere to be seen.

Jonathan proudly ushered Gudrun ahead of him into the chief ranger's office in the late morning. They had showered and changed, their clothes having been brought back from the bush camp. Gudrun smelled enticing and looked superb, with her long fair braids hanging down in front of her shoulders.

The secretary said to please wait, the chief ranger would not be long, and showed them to chairs facing the desk. Gudrun laid her precious, filthy sack on the floor beside her. As people do in an unfamiliar office, Jonathan glanced around, hoping the decor and possessions would tell them something of the person they waited for.

Behind the desk was a picture of the President and another of Nelson Mandela. Group photos of staff, as well as some framed certificates, were prominent. High-quality pictures of game at waterholes and a series taken of a rhino capture were above a wide bookcase. On the well-polished desk stood two other framed photographs, presumably of his family. A pile of paperwork sat on one side, with a much smaller stack on the other. A pen set in a carved wooden block took the central position, and on another arm of the desk was a computer keyboard and monitor.

The chief ranger introduced himself with a polite and weak smile. He was a squat man, a head shorter than Gudrun. He looked drawn and didn't appear to have had much sleep. 'Kobus van Wyk. Would you like a coffee? Some tea maybe?'

'A gallon of beer?' Jonathan joked. 'Actually we've had one already, but I think we deserve a crate.'

'Yes.' Gudrun uttered her characteristic abrupt affirmative, accompanied by a sharp nod. Jonathan had noticed she only did it with strangers, before she became comfortable with them.

Van Wyk gave a short laugh. '*Ja*, I think we need one.' He looked at his watch as he picked up the phone. 'It not too early under the circumstances. Send for three large Castles, please Anna. My account.' His gaze flicked from Gudrun to Jonathan, sadness marking his face. 'For me, it's a wake.'

Jonathan waited in silence, well aware van Wyk had also lost someone in the disaster.

'Right now, I can only say I very sorry for the terrible experience you had.' It was evident English was not his first language. 'For me, I really, truly sad about André, he was a good man, a friend, a good ranger and a good human being. He loved the animals and the bush and would get really emotional over death, unnecessary death.'

Van Wyk's voice almost broke. He swallowed. 'All of us here in the park are going to miss him. As to your French colleague, that tragic. Please correct me if I have the wrong information, but I believe it were an accident. We going to look after his wife, I just come from talking to our doctor. He been with her and given her a sedative so she can sleep and recover physically. Someone from the French embassy is coming to help her. They will arrange a flight back to France.

'We going to hold a full inquiry and interview you all, including my people, Sipho and Petros. We'll do that as soon as we can, but we not ready yet. I need to get a team together and call in someone from head office and the police. If I don't, then everyone will have to go through the questioning again. You can all stay in the camp here for no charge until we can let you go. I very sorry for the inconvenience this will cause, but I hope you understand it necessary. I heard Mr Rider is leaving. I need to go and ask him to stay for the investigation. We need everyone involved.'

'Bastard,' Jonathan muttered.

'Sorry?'

'Nothing, Kobus. It was about something else. Please go on.'

'So, how can I help right now? I should say that within half an hour of your group being forced through the fence, I was informed of the disaster. I'm sorry, but my men could do nothing to help you with those guys holding guns to your heads.'

'We understand, Kobus.'

'Also, I know nothing of the details except one of you had died. The whole story will have to come out. The Parks Board and the media will want to know every detail, and some bigwig in government will take it much further, for sure. This is an international incident and very bad for the Park's publicity. Perhaps you can give me a quick brief of what happened. It will be some background for me, and we can get into the detail later.'

'Actually, we're here for another reason,' Jonathan said.

Gudrun lifted the sack off the floor and held it out without a word.

Van Wyk took it from across the desk and peered inside. 'What you got here? Bloody hell, what …?'

The ranger listened, shaking his head every now and again, as Jonathan summarised their experience without any embellishments.

'That's a helluva story. I'd say you very brave, and you very lucky to be alive. Tell me, this stranger you saw when the village was attacked, can you describe him better?'

'It's not accurate because I only saw him in the firelight. About five-eight, one metre seventy tall, slight build with a coffee-coloured complexion. There was something oriental about him – the eyes, of course – but his other features were not entirely African, yet he had African hair.'

Anna brought in a tray with three beers and three chilled glasses. She moved the smaller pile of papers to one side and laid the tray on the desk.

'*Dankie*, Anna. I'll open them.' Kobus waited until the secretary had left the room. 'That sounds like Poh. We don't know much about him. We know his mother was from Mozambique and his father was Chinese or Vietnamese. We've always suspected he runs a horn-smuggling racket as well as ivory. He operates mainly from Moz, but I heard he's travelling further these days, to Kenya and Zambia. We've never had enough evidence to arrest him, so he comes in and out of South Africa as he wants.'

'What can we do to get him?' It was the first time Gudrun had said anything since agreeing to the beer.

Van Wyk studied her. He must have noticed the anger and determination, because he pushed his head forward and wagged his finger to emphasise what he was saying. 'You should understand Poh is a very dangerous man. He got a lot at stake that he won't want to lose, and he's suspected of several murders. You need to be careful. What are your plans from here?'

Jonathan told him what they were doing and outlined what they intended to do next, but added, 'What worries us is who we can trust. We hear so many stories of corruption in the police and the government. I'm sorry if that's offensive, but the press is always on about it.'

'No offence. Unfortunately it true. Look, most people you can trust, but some you can't and you don't know who, so it's best not to trust anyone. You need to speak to someone, you ask me first. Call me and I'll give you a honest answer: trust, don't trust, or I don't know. I'll give a friend of mine a bell, Mike Webb. He's the head honcho in a company what supplies private anti-poaching teams and other game-park security. He's the best guy to get a prosecution going, and he's always looking for stuff he can use. He's got his HQ in Nelspruit, it's on your way back. I'll ask if he can see you as soon as you leave here, okay? You tell him you can identify Poh as a person present at a horn transaction. I'm not a lawyer, so I can't tell how much weight your evidence will have. But if you want to get this man, you going to have to be available when they arrest him – if they do. Will he recognise you?'

'Hard to say. Probably not, because I saw him in the firelight, whereas we were in the dark when we left the hut.'

Van Wyk said, 'Okay, I'm sorry, but I got a helluva lot to do. I'd love to hear more detail, but it will have to wait for later. I'm sorry,' he repeated, 'but we can't stop the bloody media from invading this place, and they will want to talk to all of you. I'll do my best to keep you guys private, but I can't guarantee it. Please don't talk to the press until I've said you can, which should be tomorrow. We have to consider the French lady and André's family before the papers tell whatever story they want.'

Jonathan was lying on the bed, staring up at the thatched roof and watching Gudrun sort through her clothes. 'A mood of anticlimax is settling on me.'

'I know what you mean. We'll have to wait for the investigation to be over before we can resume our normal lives. We're going to relive the whole experience in the interviews, so I don't feel like talking it over with the others now.'

She didn't have to. With the exception of Rider, the rest of the group had already found a table in the restaurant and were avoiding the subject.

'Did everyone get some sleep?' Jonathan said as he pulled a chair out.

'For myself, I had a great shower.' Hudson gave a broad satisfied smile. 'Half the bushveld went down the drain. I think it was blocked when I finished. Then I slept like a dead man. Eesh! Now I am hungry.'

'Me too. I feel like a new person,' Claire agreed.

'Where's Mickey got to?' Kathy had her back to the door, but she kept looking around as if Rider's appearance was imminent.

'We haven't seen him since before lunch when we had a beer.' Jonathan was cautious. Gudrun was unaware of the incident with Mickey taking the sack, and she'd be furious with him for letting it happen.

The waiter came and took their orders. As he laboriously wrote them on a pad, Kobus van Wyk came up behind him, fidgeting as he waited for the man to finish.

'Gudrun, Jonathan, can I speak with you, please?'

He led them out of the restaurant to find a quiet spot. 'My friends, I very angry, I very upset.'

'What's the matter, Kobus?'

'Everything you did, all the trouble you suffered to keep those horns from the poachers. Wasted, man, wasted.'

'Why, what are you talking about?'

'They gone, they stolen from my office! Gone. Everything you did means nothing. Now some *skellum* is going to profit. Hell, man, but I'm annoyed.'

'Who? How? Your staff?'

'*Nee*, man. I don't think so, but who knows.'

'Will you find him, do you think?'

'*Ag*, I dunno. I'll skin his bloody hide, let me tell you, if I do catch him. I'm going to warn Webb that the horns are on the market, but I dunno what he can do. I wanted to let you know 'cause you been so deep into this, and also to let off some steam, as you say.'

Jonathan's suspicions arose again. 'Did you see Mickey Rider, Kobus?'

'*Ja*, he checked out earlier. I tried to persuade him to stay for the investigation, you know, but he said he had urgent business. *Ag*, we gonna get the same story from him as from all of you, so it not so important.'

PART TWO

The Expedition

16

Glass-and-metal tables glittered in reflected light under the café's overhead canopy. Wafts of warm air from the bright paving of the Piazza at the Montecasino complex offset some of winter's chill. The cold up here on the Highveld, Jonathan had decided, felt worse than the same temperature at home in England because it was so dry.

His sleeves had crept down again. From habit, he pulled them half way up his forearms, as he liked them. Sometimes the action reminded him of his father, who had always been critical, insisting it ruined his jersey and looked sloppy. Consequently he pulled them up at any opportunity, unless it was too cold.

He waved at a waiter and ordered two fresh orange juices. 'I feel guilty staying in a five-star hotel. We should be economising.'

Gudrun's white top was set off by a greyish-blue jumper. From it, her hand stretched out to cover Jonathan's. 'I think we deserve this short break in luxury, *Sœti*. If you think about it, we've gone through a hell of an experience. One of our group was murdered and another died, leaving poor Annette.

I feel terrible about her, she was devastated, and there was nothing we could do to help. We escaped with our own lives by the skin of our teeth. No, I think we deserve to relax for a couple of days.'

This was an ideal opportunity to discuss the issue burning in Jonathan's mind. He opened his mouth to reply, but shut it again. He was in his early twenties and, while mature for his age in many ways, he admitted to himself that he was a complete drip when it came to dealing with women. The trouble was that until the rhino killing, everything had gone so right with Gudrun, there had been no need for any concern.

He had never shied away from any kind of conflict before, but he had never had to face it with someone he truly loved. With Lisa, the woman his father and her parents had been so set on him marrying over a year ago, there had been some real differences of opinion which would have caused them to break up in any event. Losing Lisa as a lover was a shame, they'd got on well, but he was not broken-hearted when they fell apart. Only his pride would have suffered if she had found someone else and ditched him. So, he concluded, he had never more than liked Lisa, albeit a lot. In fact, when he told her they had no future together, he had been altogether calm and dispassionate about the whole thing. He had been relieved to be rid of the confining dungeon of a life which she offered.

But now, with Gudrun, it was entirely different. If this disagreement with her ended their relationship, he knew he would be devastated, an emotional wreck. So he had put off the discussion, hoping the issue would fade away. And because it appeared to have done so, he once again passed up the opportunity to discuss it.

'What? You were going to say something.'

'Yes, sorry. We do deserve it, but we have to move on.

We've replaced what little we lost, the main thing being a camera. This reconnaissance would be useless without photos. So now we can look at the next phase.'

It was their first day back in Johannesburg. On their drive up to the Highveld plateau from the Kruger Park, they had stopped in Nespruit for the meeting the chief ranger had set up for them. He had told them the anti-poaching company provided services to private game ranches as well as the National Parks, and was allowed to track, ambush and arrest poachers. It had more information on the poaching gangs than the official organisations, and would be much more diligent and quicker at bringing culprits to justice.

'What did you think of our meeting with Mike Webb?' Jonathan asked. 'I think I trust him, partly because Kobus said we could, but I'm not sure about the other one.'

'Marius Something-or-other. I know what you mean. I wish he hadn't been there – there was something shifty about him. I suppose Webb trusts him. It's difficult, isn't it, believing in people you don't know.'

'We don't even know if we can trust Kobus. The profits are huge in this game.'

'True, but we have to put our faith in someone, and the chief ranger should surely be the best person to start with.'

The waiter arrived with their drinks. As he bent over the table to put some paper coasters in position before placing the glasses, he blocked Gudrun's view of the tables to her right. But Jonathan could see.

'Do not get up, do not look round. Slide across to the next chair with your back in that direction,' he said.

'Why?' Gudrun did as he asked, causing the waiter to step back.

'Will there be anything else, sir?'

'No thanks, just bring the bill, please.'

'What's wrong?' said Gudrun.

'Don't turn round. Directly behind you, two tables away, is Poh. He's got a couple of oriental people with him. Pretend you're posing for me. I'm going to take a photo of him.' Jonathan stood and took some innocent pictures of the Piazza, tracking his camera round from left to right: the imitation Tuscan bell tower, the faux collapsing plasterwork opposite, and the fountain in the centre. Out of the corner of his eye, he saw Poh watching him. As Jonathan's aim came closer to him, Poh rested his cheek on his fist, distorting and hiding his face. Jonathan sat and aimed his camera at Gudrun, but focused on Poh behind her. She mocked him with silly expressions using the end of her braids to make rude signs, so he switched his focus to her instead.

Poh had a few words with his companions, then, without ordering anything, stood and walked deeper into the café, towards the casino entrance. Jonathan scraped his chair back. 'Let's go, we need to find where this vehicle hire place is, so we can take Martin and Ginny there tomorrow.'

Gudrun stood and reached for his hand. Together they walked out into the sunlight and across the Piazza to the hotel entrance. Jonathan had the distinct feeling Poh was watching them from the darker recesses of the restaurant. The man had seen Gudrun escape from the hut in Mozambique. Had he now identified her here because of her exceptional height?

Jonathan was poring over a street map which was laid out on the counter at the hotel reception, tracing a route to their destination. 'How far is this?'

'About four kilometres, sir, but it will not be good to walk. You should take a taxi. Would you like me to summon one for you?'

'We have a car, thanks. We'll leave later.' He glanced right. Poh was at the adjacent desk. Startled, Jonathan tried to appear as if he had never seen the man before. He glanced around. Standing at tables not far away were two large and fit-looking Africans. They were facing away from each other and scanning their own sector of the room. Their sweeps overlapped at Poh, where they would focus on anyone in close proximity to the man who must be their boss.

As Jonathan took in this distribution of strength, he caught Poh's narrow obsidian eyes on his own. The man held his stare for a moment before looking away, not in a submissive manner, but making it obvious that his attention was now on Gudrun, who was flicking through a magazine at a table nearby. He studied her for a few seconds, before turning back to once again engage Jonathan in brief eye contact.

'I get the feeling we've been marked,' Jonathan said as they walked away. 'Poh had a good look at you, he studied you and made certain I knew it.'

'We should phone Webb and tell him. I want the bastard arrested straight away.'

'I'm not sure he'll do that, but you're right, he needs to know.'

'That's not all. When you were talking to the receptionist, I think I saw Mickey Rider coming out of the lift. He must have seen us, because he stepped back in immediately and moved out of my sight.'

'You said, you think …?'

'I didn't get a clear look, but I've a strong feeling.'

The chief ranger's receptionist answered the phone on the third ring. A few moments' pause and Jonathan was put through.

The noise of coffee being slurped preceded his words. '*Ja, Meneer* Scott, how's it going? Everybody good?'

'We're fine, thanks, Kobus. I wanted to ask if you've found the horns …'

'No, sorry, but no. I didn't sleep last night over that. Hell, man, but I'm angry. I reckon they gone in the smugglers' system already.'

'I also wanted to tell you Poh is here in this hotel and ask what you think we should do.'

'Is he, eh? Did you speak to Mike Webb?'

'Yes, but only yesterday before we saw Poh. Webb's not in his office until later tomorrow, I've just tried. I'm also sure Poh knows who we are, he must have recognised us from that night in the village.'

There was a clink of a cup landing back in its saucer. 'That not so good. He's bad news, that man. You must take care. I think you should get out of Jo'burg as soon as you can, get out of his face. Don't let him think you're interested in him.'

'I was hoping you would say how we could get him arrested.'

'Leave it to Webb, he knows what to do when the time is right. He's got his own plan, and he needs more evidence. Your job will be as eyewitnesses when it comes to court, you can't help with an arrest.'

'Tell that to Gudrun. She's determined to get him.'

Kobus laughed. '*Ja*, I can imagine. You got a fighter there, my friend. Not joking now, you should make yourselves scarce. Don't let Poh think you're a threat. Meantime, give Webb another call and tell him this news. And Jonathan ...'

'Yes?'

'Don't talk to anybody else there, only Webb. He's got a sidekick, Marius Steenkamp, I don't know him well, but I do know he's got some bad friends.'

'Does Webb trust him?'

'I don't know, I've been meaning to ask him about that.'

17

The arrivals hall at Johannesburg's international airport was teeming early in the morning when most of the European flights landed. A mass of relatives, friends and limo drivers jostled for position at the front, eager to be the first to see and greet their own amongst the hundreds of arriving passengers who had to fight their way through a sea of luggage trolleys, hugging lovers, entire families, wheelchairs and impatient business people.

Both Gudrun and Jonathan were tall enough to see over most heads, so they stood behind the throng in a less crowded area. 'Here they come. I love those two, but I always think they're so funny, as they're almost identical. They're both short and more like brother and sister than lovers.'

Jonathan laughed, yanked up his sleeves and put his arm round Gudrun's waist, pulling her close. 'More so dwarfed by those two enormous backpacks. What do you bet me that Martin doesn't sniff as soon as he greets us?'

'Ha! I don't bet on certain losses. Why does he do that so much?'

'He suffers from allergic rhinitis, poor bugger. I hope it

doesn't get any worse while they're here.'

Ginny – petite, red-haired, lightly freckled, bespectacled with thick-framed glasses and always neat – trod immediately behind Martin, who was small, red-haired, freckle-free, bespectacled with similar heavy-framed glasses and always shambolic. He did not lack determination, however, as he pushed and shoved his way through the blockages without stopping. 'Excuse me, please. Watch out! Coming through.' In his narrow wake Ginny grabbed the space, a Red Sea of bodies closing in behind her.

She grinned up at Gudrun as they broke free. 'Your beta testers have arrived!'

Hosted at Jonathan's expense on this exploratory venture, they were expected to provide constructive criticism before the trip was opened up to the public. Jonathan had offered them this role because both he and Gudrun wanted their friends to share this experience; all they had to pay were their travel costs.

Martin sniffed. Jonathan and Gudrun laughed together.

Martin said, 'What?'

'Nothing, let's go.'

With the rental car loaded, Jonathan briefed his friends on their immediate future. 'We have two days to buy our food and anything else you need. We'll go and see the hire company tomorrow and collect the Land Rovers on Friday. Saturday, we'll drive up to Botswana. Tarred roads and an easy camp on Saturday night will give us a chance to settle into the routine.'

Jonathan smiled at his friend's eager expression. Since they had first met, Martin had supported CJ, as Jonathan was known at school, in questionable escapades. In fact many of those often illegal ventures could not have been done without his support. Now they were embarking on a serious expedition which was well beyond anything they had experienced before.

Once they were settled in the hotel and enjoying a mid-morning coffee, Jonathan became serious. 'We need to tell you everything that happened to us in Mozambique.'

Gudrun's sharp look and shake of her head signalled she didn't want him to put the couple off and send them home, because their trip would suffer. The longer they stayed, the greater the chance of getting Poh arrested. Concern for others did not feature in her determination to succeed, and the disagreement Jonathan feared festered on the horizon. But he wasn't going to be put off; he couldn't, this had to be done, so he ignored her. Ginny stared at him in horror as the story unfolded, but Martin lapped up the tale with an almost schoolboy attitude.

'I'm telling you this because Poh is here in this hotel and has noted both of us. We're told he's a dangerous man, and may suspect we saw him that night and could be witnesses to his involvement. If he associates you with us, you too might be in some danger. We'll be out of here and on our way by the weekend, though, so I don't think there's anything to worry about. If you want to drop out, you should say so. Having you along is a luxury for us – great company – but we don't want you to feel obliged to join us. I should have told you this before you left yesterday, but honestly, I was busy and didn't think of it.'

Martin shook his head and reached for Ginny's hand. 'You can't get rid of us that easily, this will be the trip of a lifetime. Bugger Poh!'

Ginny had always been supportive of Martin and Jonathan, but managed to inject a bit of common sense into their ventures after she'd considered all the options.

'If it's so serious, why don't you leave, get out of Poh's way?'

'Because this trip is important. We've invested a lot of

money in it and it's the start of our future. We're not going to be put off. As I said, we'll be out of sight in a couple of days anyway.'

Ginny took a moment to answer. 'You know what, Jonathan? We had a little confession session on the aeroplane last night.'

Martin gave a short laugh. 'After a couple of wines.'

'They helped. We agreed that, as a pair of aerodynamicists, we are both first-class nerds. Without your spirit of adventure we would be sitting behind our computers, trying to design an aerofoil, a wing, which will have better lift and higher speed than anything out there. We would go to bed with headaches from staring at a monitor all day and be bored out of our minds in a couple of years without some kind of stimulation. You're providing something unique in this trip, and we value that for our mental and physical health more than anything.

'In any case, I don't think we're a threat to Poh from what you say. We were not in the village, we never saw him there. We're useless as witnesses, so why would he bother with us? I'm not going to miss out on this.'

'You're wrong on two counts,' Jonathan said. 'Nerds are single-minded, you're not. Single-minded aerodynamicists are not adventurous, you are. So therefore I class you both as geniuses. Geniuses can be adventurous, can't they?'

'Genius is a bit strong, but I never liked being a nerd. Reclassification gratefully accepted, thank you,' said Martin and sniffed again.

Back in their room, after Ginny and Martin had gone for a nap to catch up on the sleep they missed on the overnight flight, Gudrun vented her opinion. 'You didn't have to tell them everything that happened. Hearing it all, they might have backed out.'

'First, Gudrun, I know Martin, he wouldn't back out.'

'Ginny might have, she's more sensible.'

Jonathan ignored her comment. 'Second, we have to give our clients a truthful explanation of the risks involved in anything we do. Not only is it fair, but we could also be sued if anything happened to them and we hadn't told them what they were in for. I'm sorry, but you can be reckless, which I admire to some extent, but we cannot have our friends now, or our clients in the future, put in a situation they did not sign up for. Think, Gudrun, how will you feel if a third party is hurt or dies because you did something which put them in danger? We need to have this out now, because our future in this venture hangs on agreement between us. This is serious.'

Her glare pinned him to the spot. Her cheeks were flushed. 'You don't get it, do you? I'm going to get him. Nothing is going to stop me from getting Poh convicted. If Ginny and Martin had backed out, our trip would be off and we would go home. How would I then get Poh?'

'That's not true, our trip would not be off, we'd go ahead with it as planned. In any case, I told you they wouldn't back down.'

Gudrun broke her stare and strode over to the window. Jonathan waited, his stomach churned. Would she stand up to him and a rift develop between them? The ramrod stiffness of her posture articulated her mood.

Five whole long minutes passed. At last she turned and came towards him. She looked down at him. He studied her, not in anger, more trying to determine where this was going to end; neither blinked. He was not going to back down on this, he couldn't. Her face softened, her voice was a murmur. 'I'm sorry. I cannot stop my anger at that man. But you're right.' A pause. 'Jonathan ...'

His heart was going to burst with relief. 'Yes?' he croaked.

'Take me. Now. Don't be gentle.'

* * *

The owner of Thor Expeditions was well over sixty years old. His face had been tanned for decades, maybe since birth, and had the texture of aniline leather. Once pale hair now barely existed. Washed-out blue eyes and his halting English indicated his origins were probably from the old German colony of South West Africa. He was dressed as if he was going into the bush, in a green and khaki shirt and long khaki trousers. It was all part of the outdoor image the staff in such shops liked to project. He welcomed the four of them into his office, introduced himself as Günter Mueller, ordered coffee and indicated they take seats at a large table. Spreading out a map of Botswana, he said, 'Right, tell me where you going.'

As Jonathan spoke with his finger tracing across the map, Martin and Ginny leaned forward to see, but the old man's glance kept flicking to Gudrun. When she looked at him, he grinned impishly.

'Well, we don't know the country at all, but we want to join Hunter's Road on the Zimbabwe border after Nata and go all the way up to Kasane and Kazungula. Across on the ferry and see Victoria Falls, then back across the north of Botswana to Caprivi, and head for northern Namibia, where we'll start phase two of our journey. We would like your advice, of course.'

Günter nodded pleasantly as he recalled his own adventures. 'Good trip. I have been everywhere there, but in many trips, not one. Sure, I can help. Now, I can give you Land Rovers or Mercedes G-Wagens. I will make more money from the G-Wagen, but the Landy is more comfortable and more capable. Also, spares are more available. The cars are fully kitted out, all you need is food.' He winked. 'And something strong to keep you going.'

They knuckled down to negotiating the price, with Jonathan explaining how they would be back with tourists in the future if all went well, and maybe they could do a regular business together. Mueller's face lit up with amusement and the enjoyment of a little bargaining. They flicked again to Gudrun. 'I like you guys. You'll get good support from me. Any trouble, you get on the phone and I'll deal with it. Excuse me,' he said, and shouted, 'Moses.'

An assistant came in after knocking on the door. 'Sah?'

'Moses, these good people are taking two Land Rovers up to Botswana. I want you to make sure they equipped with everything they need. They not from South Africa, so they don't want to be let down in the bush because something was forgotten from your lists, okay? They leave on Saturday.'

Moses beamed. 'No problem, Mistah Günter. I'll do it.'

Günter turned back to Jonathan. 'The cars have extra fuel tanks, both will be full, also two cans each. We fit special water tanks and they be filled when you pick them up. Also there a small fridge in each car. As you saw, there spotlights mounted on the roof rack, and there plenty of tie-downs and cargo straps so you can keep your kit from falling off the top.' He laughed. 'Come on Friday and load your food and kit. I show you and your friends around the cars and make sure all's good. Personal service with Moses here to help – he's an expert. He's going to be doing nothing else but getting your cars ready for you.'

They shook hands on the deal prior to leaving, but Günter insisted on joining them back at the hotel, where they would have a couple of beers. He seemed keen to offer his advice and share his vast experience with them. He had been giving Gudrun puzzled glances throughout the visit, a fact that had not escaped Jonathan. By the time he left, Günter could not contain himself and said, 'I seen you before, I'm sure of it. You play tennis?'

She gave him a warm glance. 'No, but I'm asked that a lot.'

* * *

From behind the dark tinted window of a black Toyota Land Cruiser which was parked in the street, a large, fit and muscle-bound African watched the five leave the office. He pulled a wad of notes out of his wallet, tucked them into his shirt pocket and went into reception.

<h1 style="text-align:center">18</h1>

In the afternoon, Jonathan stopped the hire car at traffic lights at the junction of Witkoppen Road and Main to the north of Johannesburg. It was stuffy in the closed vehicle, and the air conditioning was not coping with the four people inside. To open the window would be against the security advice he had been given: keep them closed when stopped to prevent thieves from grabbing at your possessions. So he made sure they were all up. There were no vehicles in the adjacent lane for the right turn, and he was at the front of his queue. Behind was a big black pickup. He didn't take any notice of it, his attention too focused on the traffic light opposite while he waited for the green. Gudrun was head down delving in the bag between her knees. In the back, Ginny and Martin were poring over a map. None of them saw the two men approach from behind, one on either side of the car.

A hard pointed object like a spark plug held in the fist and driven with great force at a flat side window shatters it. The fist follows through in a smooth movement and snatches the mobile phone, wallet, handbag or purse. Then, as quickly as it was thrust in, the hand is whipped out and the goods are gone, the thief diving through the traffic for the safety and cover of the trees.

It was not like that. But it was incredibly fast. The joint impacts, the shower of little diamonds of glass on both sides as the windows burst with almost simultaneous cracks, stunned them for a moment. A pistol was rammed through each hole. Jonathan's right eye looked straight into the muzzle. Gudrun's head was pushed over by the gun at her temple. Ginny yelped in surprise and fright. Martin gasped. An engine screamed behind them. A crunch, a thump and Jonathan's door was hit. The car rocked. The arm and the gun were dragged out of his window as the man vanished below the sill. The thief was on all fours for a few paces, scrabbling to get away. On his feet, he limped as fast as he could to the far side of the road. A screech of brakes from another car, and he escaped. On the left, Gudrun's robber was pushed off balance and ran, vaulting over a bonnet and jumping over a drain.

'You all right?' A stocky, fair and curly-haired man was peering through the broken window.

Jonathan tried to open his door. It was stuck. He pushed again, and the man pulled on the handle. Two tugs and it gave way. Jonathan squeezed out and around the man's 4x4, which was immediately behind his dented door. He was confused as to what had happened, but saw a massive bill and a fight with the hire company looming on the horizon. 'What the hell?'

The blond man regarded him calmly, waiting for a reaction. The lights changed and impatient horns sounded from the back of the queue. Other lines of traffic moved forward. The black pickup reversed and switched into the next lane to pass them.

Jonathan shook his head as if to clear it. 'Did you just run him down?'

'Man, did you not see the gun at your head? You were a split second from being killed. I've seen it before and I am NOT going to see it again if I can do anything about it.' He leaned down to see into the car. Gudrun hadn't moved. Ginny had her hand on Gudrun's shoulder, and Martin was getting out. 'You okay in there?' the man said.

'I'm sorry.' Jonathan held out his hand. 'You saved our lives. Sorry, it all happened so fast, I've just realised what you did. Thanks, thanks.'

'Hey, no problem. You look like you could do with a beer or two. There's a pub round the corner. Follow me and we'll sort this out over a cold one, okay?'

It was early, too early for those having a drink on the way home from work, so there were no delays to Jonathan's beer order.

'Angus,' the man said as he introduced himself and laughed. 'Angus Pennington. My dad descended from the 1820 settlers, and my mother was Scottish but born here, so I'm a thoroughbred South African.'

They sorted out the damage to the hire car. Angus said his cousin was the financial director of the hire company, and he would get the excess waived. Jonathan protested, saying he had saved their lives. Angus responded, 'Hey, you're guests in our beautiful country, and we don't want you to leave with a bad taste in your mouth. There are plenty of good people here of all colours. Those guys, they're drugged-up scum that work in gangs. It's organised crime, man, organised.'

'But did you have to drive into him? You might have killed him,' Ginny said, her voice higher pitched than normal.

'Huh!' Angus scoffed.

The casual and almost rude reaction to a natural question was surprising. Jonathan tried to see his group from Angus's perspective. Ginny: bobbed red hair, the black T-shirt offsetting creamy white skin which had seldom been exposed to the sun, and black-rimmed spectacles which added to the innocence in her face. A girl from the First World, she and Martin were people who had never experienced violence, and Angus might think she even dreaded reading about it. And these two had only arrived that morning – what a welcome!

Jonathan looked at Gudrun. She was silent, grim and determined at that moment, brooding on something. Was she in shock, or was it something else? And himself? What did Angus think of him?

Angus appeared to recognise the gulf between the tourists' attitude to the event and his own. 'Sorry if I sound harsh, but in the last year I've seen two of my friends robbed. In their homes, at night, tied up with wire and beaten. All their things were taken: computers, TV, money, phones, you name it. Five months ago, a man I knew was at home in bed with his wife. He heard a noise and got up. He was pulling on his jeans when a guy sticks a gun through the window and shoots him. BANG! Dead!' He smacked his hand down on the table in anger, and Ginny jumped. 'Just like that – dead!'

He took a deep breath as if to recover his temper. 'You have a safe country, so I guess it's hard to understand. Last week, my wife was in the supermarket. Two guys come in with AKs – bloody sub-machine guns! They come and everybody's down on the floor, and they take the money from the tills. No, man, people are running out of patience in this place. Of the people I know, all of them have either been robbed or know someone who has experienced the same thing, or been killed. The police either don't know what to do about it, or can't, or won't do anything – maybe some are even involved. My wife is still upset. So, can you understand why I get angry?'

No one responded. Angus took a sip of beer and went on. 'I saw that guy go to your window, and I thought I knew what he was going to do. Then I saw the gun, and I had to do something. Believe me, Ginny, I'm not trying to take credit here, but if I had not run him down and Jon here had made the slightest wrong move, he would now be dead.' His words were uttered with such deep feeling, it was impossible to disregard his attitude.

Martin broke the silence which followed. 'Thanks, Angus. We owe you our lives. Should we report this to the police?'

The South African laughed. 'Forget it, you'll waste your time. Even if they try, they'll never catch them. Another beer?'

'No, this one's on me,' Gudrun said. 'There was a gun to my head too.' She waved at the waiter, and looked again at Angus. 'Is there any chance we were targeted?'

Angus regarded her for a long time before answering. 'You two are not so shocked.'

'We've been through our own spot of trauma recently,' Jonathan explained. 'You were going to answer whether we were targeted.'

Angus nodded. 'Those guys operate by walking up and down the queue of cars until they see a good target, then they do their thing and run. I'm not sure, because I wasn't watching, but I think they jumped out of a bakkie, a pickup, behind you. If that was so, then maybe you're right and you were followed. On the other hand that crossing is a hot-spot; there are trees for cover on all sides. Even the police warn about it. Why you ask?'

Gudrun shook her head.

Jonathan saw Angus was pleased with himself. He was reluctant to leave, but after the second beer he had to go.

'God! He's intense,' said Ginny after he'd left. 'Do you think his attitude is wide spread? It's a sad reflection if it is.'

'From what I've heard,' Jonathan said, 'a lot of people may think like that but would never do anything about it. He sounds like a man who has experienced more than his fair share of crime and has simply had enough. He might be a bit of a vigilante. They're a small minority in any country.'

The others fell silent for a while, letting their lucky escape sink in and the excitement subside. There was still tension in the group, though, and tempers were short.

Jonathan was the first to break the silence. He said to Gudrun, 'I think you're right that we were targeted by Poh.'

Ginny put her drink down and sat back. 'Don't you think you're being a bit paranoid over the man?'

Gudrun's words were sharp. 'Of course it was him. Who else would it be?'

'There's no need to bite my head off, Gudrun.'

Gudrun stared at nothing for a moment, then put a hand on Ginny's arm. 'Sorry. Of course not. I'm just bloody angry. I don't like having a gun to my head, and that man, that …'

Jonathan said, 'If it was an attempt at theft, immediately after the glass broke there would have been a hand in the window, grabbing at something. That didn't happen, so I think it was an attempt to kill us, or maybe kidnap us.'

'Precisely,' Gudrun snapped.

'And the only way they could have targeted us was to have followed us, and the only way they could be close was to be in a vehicle behind us.'

'Exactly.'

Jonathan drained his beer. 'Look, whether it was Poh or not, he could have been behind it, and that's the point. He's a serious threat, and we had better be extra careful from now on. Keep your eyes open for cars or people that might be following us.'

Martin pulled a handkerchief from his pocket. 'In two days we'll be out of this place and heading north. When Poh sees us go, he might ignore us,'

'He might, he might not. We can still give evidence.'

'Why don't you go to the police?'

'We told you what the chief ranger said: there's so much corruption, don't trust anyone. You heard what Angus said a moment ago. And Poh has lots of money and a long reach. By going to the wrong person, we could be creating a trap for ourselves. No, I think the best thing is to get out of Jo'burg as planned and disappear into the bush.'

Jonathan glanced at Gudrun, who was staring at her beer in silence. He understood the fury and frustration she felt at not being able to do anything about Poh, but he had to keep her under control.

'Gudrun, I don't understand. Why do you want to nail this gangster when you're up against such a dangerous man? We've seen what he's capable of.'

'Ginny, you have to make a stand about something if you believe it's wrong. If nobody did anything about the things we believe in, we would not progress as a human race, and we won't have a world worth living in.'

'But Iceland still hunts whales,' Martin commented.

'Yes, and that is also wrong. In the old days subsistence hunting was okay, but we don't live in the old days any more, and to hunt whales or elephants or rhinos purely for profit is wrong, and I will oppose it in any way I can. In Iceland exported fin whale meat is sold to Japan, and the meagre profit goes into a company which clings to tradition for no good reason and might have friends in the government. Minke whales are killed by another company for local consumption. Most people oppose it these days, but they don't do anything. I can't accept that, I won't accept it, and it's the same with this poor rhino. Some humans have to fight for the animals, so I'm willing to take the risk on myself and get this bloody murderer. At least with the whale something is done with the carcass, but with the rhino, the body is left to rot; they don't eat it. Killing a rhino for its horn is all about money, and that is *so* wrong.'

'How far are you prepared to go?' Jonathan said. 'There's a

lot of risk involved.'

'I know I have a responsibility to protect our world from ourselves. I'm angry not everyone feels this way, and because they don't I have to go even further to make up for their deficiencies. I will go all the way, Jonathan. I have to take a stand, so nothing is going to stop me from convicting Poh. If you haven't got the stomach for it then we have a serious difference between us.'

'Calm down, Gudrun, we're on the same side. I want to get him as much as you do, but I'm not prepared to put third parties at risk in this fight.'

'Huh.' Gudrun strode off to the bathroom.

'She's vehement, Jonathan. How do you feel about it?'

'I only gave it a passing thought before, Ginny. But having witnessed that appalling rhino killing, I now feel the same way. We have to do something to stop these people. The difference between Gudrun and me is she's impetuous, whereas I will plan. She gets impatient with me, and angry, but we'll pull together when the time comes.'

Gudrun returned in a better mood, and gave them all an amiable look. 'You were talking about me, weren't you? No matter. I want to add something else. Poh attacked us today. He tried to kill us. He needs to understand we will not run away from him. He now has a fight on his hands, because nothing turns out for the better by giving in.'

19

'Steenkamp.'

'May I speak to Mike Webb, please? It's Jonathan Scott here.'

'Ah, Mister Scott, good morning. Mike is a bit busy right now, can I help you? I'm fully in the picture.'

'Yes, I'm sure, but I think I should speak to Mike himself when he's available, if you don't mind.'

'Let me see if he can take your call.'

There was a click and too long a pause. Jonathan was about to put the receiver down and call again, when Webb said, 'Good morning, Jonathan. How can I help you?'

'Poh is here in the hotel, and he made it obvious he knows who we are. Not only that, but we're sure he attempted to kill us yesterday afternoon – a carjacking.'

As Jonathan told the story and listened to Webb's response, Gudrun was studying him – trouble was on the horizon.

'No, we can't prove it was his doing, but we're sure we were targeted, and there's no one else who has a reason to kill us. There's one other thing: Kobus told you the horns have been stolen, didn't he?'

'Yes.'

'Well, Mickey Rider tried to hide them from me, perhaps as a prelude to taking them. He then checked out and left the park. Gudrun thinks she saw him in reception here yesterday when we saw Poh. Draw your own conclusions.'

Gudrun had thrust her head forward at him, her look growing more intense as he spoke. Jonathan swallowed – *here it comes*.

He put the phone down. 'Webb won't move yet,' he said in as normal a voice as he could, since he was about to go on the defensive. 'He doesn't have a watertight case and insists we stay well out of it until he needs us. He said we should get away from here; leave the country preferably, or on our trip as soon as possible.'

'What do you mean, Rider tried to hide the horns? Why didn't you tell me this?'

He cleared his throat and told her what happened.

'Why are you only telling me this now? Was this a secret? Understand me: secrets are not acceptable. There must be no secrets between us, Jonathan. Do you have more?'

'There are no more secrets, I promise. I didn't tell you because you were tired, not in a good mood, and I feared another argument. I thought he might be playing a joke on me, so it wasn't important. I'm sorry.'

'No more secrets?'

'None, I promise.'

Gudrun dropped her imprisoning glare and paced up and down, venting her frustration in her own language. 'Can we trust Webb? Is he going to do something or is this a bluff to keep us out of the way?'

'You tell me that first impressions count. What did they tell you about Webb when we met him?'

'I liked him, I think we can trust him, but I have been wrong sometimes.'

'Agreed. I think he's all right, but we don't know if he is. I do think the sooner we are out of Poh's sight the better, for now at least. When Webb is in a position to arrest him, that's the time to take some action. I'm thinking of Martin and Ginny.'

Gudrun pursed her lips, but said nothing.

In their room a little later, Gudrun vented her frustrations. 'Jonathan. I can't stand doing nothing. Because he has no scruples, Poh will do what he likes. We do care, and we don't want to break the law, therefore he has a big advantage. He has already tried to kill us once, and now we are waiting for him to try again. I won't accept this.'

'I know what you mean, but I can't think what to do about it.'

'We need to be aggressive. He will not expect that.'

'I hear you, and I don't disagree. What do you think we should do?'

'Make Webb arrest him would be best.'

'You heard me calling Webb again. They're not yet ready to take that step. If he doesn't get it right, if he doesn't get enough evidence, the case will fall apart. The best thing to do is get out of the way, let Webb gather his evidence and then come back to hit at Poh when we have Webb's support. Right now, Webb considers us a liability – he probably thinks you're an unexploded bomb that could wreck his whole case.'

'He has no idea how right he is. If no one else is going to do anything, we must do something ourselves.' Her tone was rising. Jonathan knew if he didn't calm her down they were going to have another row.

'Meaning?'

'Do something to him, frighten him so he leaves us alone. Maybe capture him and threaten him or expose him to a great danger.'

'Now you're being silly. We'll never get past those two musclemen I saw in reception. I'll bet there's one sitting outside his room all night. And even if we did, Poh is not the sort to give in. No matter what promises he makes, he'll break them, and we still won't be any better off.'

'Why are you being so negative?'

Jonathan shared her frustration at the lack of options. Hers were reaching a peak, however. 'I'm not being negative. I'm trying to think of something effective and practical to do. There's no point rushing in without thinking our plan through.'

'What happened to the risk-taking, devil-may-care man I met?' she mocked. 'Are you following your father's doctrine: take no risks, think safety, safety, safety?' Shaking her head, she sneered, 'Blah, blah, blah …'

The reference to his dominant health-and-safety-conscious father, with his painful and stifling concerns over risks, irritated Jonathan. 'No, I'm not following my dad's example. I never have done. I've always calculated the risks I've taken and seldom done something stupid.'

'Oh, so I'm not only reckless, I'm stupid, am I?'

It was Jonathan's turn to be angry. 'Don't be ridiculous. You're far from stupid, but you are hot-headed, reckless and casual with other people's lives.'

'Don't start that again!' she shouted, and stormed into the bathroom, slamming the door.

Jonathan searched through the minibar for a whisky. He hated this division which had grown between them. The only arguments they'd had up until then were inconsequential. Even so, any disagreement felt like another cut into their otherwise perfect relationship. Too many cuts and the tree would topple. They were also becoming more frequent as Gudrun became more impatient. The tension between them was rising, but she didn't care. Her whole focus was on Poh.

Everything else, including himself, was a separate issue. To her, their relationship was not connected to the real and dangerous problem which faced them as a couple. And he hadn't a clue as to how to solve any of it.

He took the only two miniature bottles on the shelf and poured each one into a glass. Gudrun soon came out. Without a word he handed her one of the drinks. 'Cheers.'

Her eyes were red-rimmed and bloodshot. She wiped tears of exasperation off her cheeks and took the Scotch. '*Skål*. You know how to fix me.' Her face softened. 'I'm sorry, again. I get so angry at being unable to do anything, and you're right, there's nothing we can do which would be effective, even if we did get close to the bastard. But don't think I've given in.'

'Nothing was further from my mind.'

Jonathan relaxed, but not fully. Her anger had surfaced again, and for the second time she had backed down when he had told her how futile it was and how selfish she was being. But the anger had not gone away. Although she had tried, she had not been able to control it on her own. When it rose she was capable of doing foolish and dangerous things. She cared nothing of the risks to herself or anyone else. If she couldn't keep her rage under control, what kind of future, if any, would they have together? He wasn't even sure she listened to a word he said when she was in this frame of mind, and, little by little, her selfishness was driving a wedge between them. It was hurting him, but she was oblivious to his pain, which hurt him even more. Again the doubts crept into his mind and, lying there amongst all the good and positive thoughts, they began their insidious corruptive process.

Thursday passed in a flash, it seemed. They spent it completing their lists of equipment and clothing suitable for the bush: medicines, sun cream, insect repellent, environmentally-friendly washing powder, food, beer and other drinks – all of which were obtainable through the proliferation of outdoor shops and supermarkets in northern Johannesburg.

At last Friday came around and they collected the cars. Günter Mueller was enthusiastic in his support for the group and voluble in his advice.

'You know, some people would laugh at you going into the bush with no experience. It's wild and can be tough. But you guys remind me of myself as a youngster up there in South West – Namibia. All the old people tried to tell me how bad it could be if something went wrong, but I wanted to go and see for myself, so I did. You guys are keen, and you act professional. I know you understand, so good luck and you must call if you need help. I'll organise. All right?'

In their loaded vehicles, the two couples left Thor Expeditions for their last night of luxury in a five-star hotel. Günter waved them off. Moses stood alongside him, grinning from ear to ear.

20

The camping ground at Martin's Drift on the Limpopo appealed to them all. Once through Botswana immigration, they searched for a spot to set up for the night.

'There's a good place.' Jonathan pointed. 'We'll get two vehicles under the trees.'

'And there's a good view of the river,' Gudrun said.

With stops, it had taken them under six hours to reach the border. For the whole trip there had been a black Toyota Land Cruiser on the same route. When they stopped, Jonathan noticed it too pulled up beside the road, but a good distance away. It had never come close until it joined the queue for immigration two cars behind Martin. Now, as they discussed the camping arrangements, Jonathan saw what could have been the same vehicle drive slowly past them and disappear behind some trees, looking for another site.

There was nothing strange about a Land Cruiser, it was a popular model, although most were of a light colour to fight off the heat. Besides, dozens of people followed this route into Botswana. If he told Gudrun, she would get angry and might challenge the occupants. As he didn't want to alarm the other two, he kept quiet. Suspicion would not leave him alone, though, the carjacking ensured that.

Günter Mueller had given them a thorough briefing on the camping equipment in his vehicles: the roof-top tent on each Land Rover, the ladder to reach them, the cooking appliances, water tank, camping shower, everything. This was their first attempt to try it all out and learn for future nights. Mistakes were made, but they muddled through over a few beers and laughed a lot. Well after dark, while they were sitting around a fire, Jonathan explained the next day's route.

His finger traced across the map. 'This is the route to Nata where we'll pick up the A33, the main road north to Zambia. After another hour, we'll branch off onto a track. Nata's about four hundred and fifty kilometres away. I think we should get the paved-road driving behind us as soon as possible so we can move into the bush free of the traffic.'

After another, but better organised, night at Nata, they filled up with fuel in the morning and moved on. A further sixty kilometres later they came to the veterinary check point at Ngwasha where they had to drive through a shallow dip of disinfectant, put there to combat the spread of foot and mouth disease. As Jonathan moved his car forward to allow Martin to have his turn with the inspectors, he saw a black Land Cruiser once again stopping behind his friend. Leaving Gudrun in the car, he walked back to the inspection point, hoping to see who was in the Toyota, but it had heavily tinted windows.

Jonathan leaned on Martin's door. 'I'm going to slow down soon. The access to Hunter's Road is supposed to be a nondescript branch to the right about four kilometres further on.'

To Gudrun a moment later, he said, 'There's been a black Land Cruiser behind us all the way from Jo'burg. It was in the campsite last night as well.'

She frowned and turned to look behind. He saw her readying for battle.

'*No*, stop,' she said to herself, but out loud, and relaxed. She lifted her chin and gave him a broad, satisfied grin. 'Did it. Proud of me?'

'Very.'

'Are you going to tell the others?'

'Not at the moment, it's probably nothing. Let's see what happens when we leave the main road.'

The turn-off wasn't difficult to identify, and they left the tarred surface for a sand track exactly where Günter had described it to be. Jonathan pulled up a little way into the bush and watched the Land Cruiser continue along the tarred road to the north.

'We've about twenty kilometres to go to get to Ngwahla Pan, which is on the Zimbabwe border. We want to set up camp somewhere suitable near there. It's not so far, but we don't know what the going is like or how slow we have to travel. We've plenty of time, and there's no point in rushing it. With a bit of luck we'll see lots of game.'

The track was more or less straight, passing through thin, desiccated, khaki-coloured grass and scattered low trees and bushes which, at that time of year, were a mixture of brown and green. The occasional larger tree, with a more luxurious growth, stood out from the rest. The vehicles were able to keep up a steady pace on the soft surface. At first Jonathan strove to keep the car straight, as the sand ruts held the wheels in their grip and yanked the vehicle from side to side, while keeping it on the track. His efforts were pointless, so he let the sand have its way, only correcting its more erratic attempts to take control.

Game paths led off into the bush in places. 'Where are they going to, or coming from? Some must lead to water, surely?'

Gudrun said.

'We're following a slight depression. Maybe it floods in the rains in places, and these are the paths the animals use to go there every evening.'

They passed a man-made water point, a small concrete dam with a wind pump above it. Soon afterwards they rose out of the shallow riverbed and followed the dead-straight track to a junction. Jonathan stopped, and they all got out to stretch their legs. He spread a map out over the engine. 'I reckon this is where we branch off to the right.'

Martin agreed. 'Yes, we should now follow another riverbed to the border and the pan. It's about ten kilometres – less.'

At the sound of an engine, they all looked up at and saw a light aircraft passing overhead. 'It's a Cessna 172, like Dad's,' said Martin. 'That brings back a few happy memories, eh?'

'And one not so pleasant.' Jonathan was thinking about his crash in Terry's aeroplane, brought about by Barry Castle, who was now serving a lengthy sentence.

'Have you been doing any flying since then?'

'I kept at it, as you know, and got my licence. But having left home and embarked on this career, I haven't had either the time or the opportunity. Pity – I don't want to give it up, I still want to gain more experience and get good at it. What about you?'

Martin sniffed and pulled out his handkerchief. 'Oh, I keep current, under my dad's watchful eye, of course.'

'I wonder where he's going.' Gudrun was still staring at the little aircraft. 'He's heading towards Zimbabwe. No, he's turning north.'

'Maybe he's looking for game, there are hunting areas further on,' Ginny said.

Jonathan folded the map. 'Maybe. Let's get going and find a place to camp.'

Ngwahla Pan proved to be a shallow depression, with the only sign of moisture at that time of year a sludge which had the consistency of marzipan. It was obvious, though, that it did fill in during the wet season, because there were plenty of animal tracks in the dried mud at the edge. About half of it was in Zimbabwe and the rest in Botswana. Hunter's Road, an unremarkable sand track, followed the western edge of the pan in a northerly direction. They found some shade under a couple of big trees a short distance away.

The Cessna passed overhead once more at about a thousand feet before turning west.

Gudrun watched it disappearing. 'What do you think? Connected to your Land Cruiser?'

'I don't know. It might be game-spotting, but it might be a security flight watching the border or something like that.'

'You want to tell them?'

'I think we should, don't you?'

Gudrun smiled and nodded.

A beautiful evening. A rose tint to the earth as the sun departed behind a dusty horizon. A clear sky for the night ahead. They set up their barbecue and brought out their meat. Martin declared himself barman, for the first round anyway. Ginny came out of her shell and started a trend with a funny story about her time at university. It was perfect relaxation.

For Martin and Ginny, who had only heard about Mozambique and the trauma the other two had endured there, the possibility of trouble, of criminal involvement, was remote. When Gudrun – laughing to Jonathan that it was her little penance – told the couple of their suspicions that they were being watched, it was easy for the pair to put it to one side and let Jonathan worry about it. For the man himself and Gudrun, however, it was a serious matter, and they did not sleep soundly. Was there a connection between a black car and a light aircraft?

The night was uneventful and, with the dawn, the worries of the dark receded. After some strong coffee and a light breakfast, they packed up and made ready to leave. Martin wandered down to the edge of the pan. He called out, 'Come and look at this.'

An enormous paw print had been left in the soft mud. 'That was not here when I came down yesterday afternoon, I would have seen it. See, those are my footprints over there. It must be a lion, last night,' he said, with a nervous glance into the bush.

Ginny studied the print. 'It's definitely a cat, and there's nothing else with paws that size. I think we should get back in the vehicles.'

'Relax,' said Jonathan. 'Gudrun will glare it down, or tackle it with her bare hands.'

Gudrun laughed and pulled him up to the Land Rover.

'Seriously guys, that paw print is a lesson. Keep your eyes open. Look around carefully before you get out of the car and don't stray far from it,' Jonathan said when they reached the vehicles. 'If you can't see into the bush, wait until there's a clear patch and you're able to.'

The route was sandy, but easy going most of the way. To their right was Hwange National Park in Zimbabwe, but there was neither a border nor a game fence. The animals had learned the difference between the hunting concessions in Botswana and the game reserve in Zimbabwe.

They motored along, taking their time, enjoying the wildness and peace of the area. The scene was pretty, and giant anthills – red mud stalagmites – were a cause to stop and photograph the six-foot two-inch Gudrun and the five-foot three-inch Ginny looking up at their summits until they became bored of posing.

Their peace was disturbed by the noise of a light aircraft heading north. Jonathan glanced at it and at Gudrun. She shrugged her shoulders.

In the afternoon they reached the junction where the cutline which divides the North West District from the Central District met the road. Dead straight, the cutline headed due west to meet the A33, some thirty kilometres away. They moved on to find a camping spot at the edge of another pan where the greenery was thicker and provided some shade.

The aircraft came back in a southerly direction. It was much lower this time, but it flew past without appearing to notice them.

Set back from the pan were some large trees with adequate space between them to park the two Land Rovers side by side to form a social area. There was still a couple of hours until darkness would envelop them, but there was little point in going further and then fumbling around to pitch camp by torchlight. They had had enough of driving for the day anyway.

Martin appreciated Jonathan's determination for the trip not to be about meeting schedules or setting targets, but about relaxing in the wild. He wanted to experience the fullness of nature, which was not achievable while sitting in a vehicle. He had discussed it with Ginny. They agreed they needed to be able to hear the sounds of the bush: birds, rustles in the grass and the occasional grunt of something unseen. They wanted to feel the breeze, smell the dust and see what wildlife might come their way.

Setting up camp was much quicker that night, and Martin delivered the beers at least half an hour earlier than before.

A lion roared, a blood-chilling sound to anyone, more so to these inexperienced explorers.

'Wow,' Martin said. 'That was powerful. How far away do you think it was?'

Jonathan sipped his beer and smacked his lips. 'I haven't a clue. Sound carries.'

'I think we should make a fire. It might keep Leo away.'

'Be careful. The last thing we want to do is start a wildfire.'

Ginny said, 'It's too risky. The slightest spark will light this grass, it's so dry.'

Gudrun agreed. 'Ginny's right. It will be better if we pack up the food and talk from the top of our vehicles. You can take your beer to bed, Martin.'

'How many am I allowed?'

'Fill your sandals.'

They chatted until eleven. Martin, keen for another round, climbed down his ladder to get to the fridge. 'The beer'sh not going to last at thish rate.'

'Then we'll have to switch to whisky,' Jonathan said.

Martin handed two beers up to Gudrun and began the climb to his own tent, but his foot slipped on the bottom step and he fell against the ladder with his face between the rungs.

'You know, you're right,' he said before he extricated himself. 'I'm not a true nerd. Nerds are too intense to get pished. There's no doubt I'm a geniush; geniae are super-intelligent, but are short on common shensh. I'm going to sleep here. The geniush at the bottom of the ladder, thash me.'

'Martin!' Ginny's voice was sharp. 'Put those beers back and get up here now. You've had enough, and it's not safe down there.'

'A lion wouldn't want to eat a pished geniush, Ginny darling. Lions don't like beer.'

'Martin Beale!'

Gudrun and Jonathan's affectionate laughter rang out.

Some time before two, Martin had a desperate need. He

squinted at his watch but without his glasses couldn't read it. Whatever time it was, he would have to go out to relieve himself. Not bothering to put on any more than his underpants, he found his sandals and clambered down the short ladder, taking great care not to let his foot slip again.

He moved away from the trees onto the clear ground of the road, where he would be able to see if something was stalking him, and gasped in relief at his first release. With the pressure off, his fuddled brain was able to focus on his exposed situation. He was standing in the middle of the track, alone and almost naked in the chill of the night. A weird feeling of freedom enveloped him, but it made him aware of his vulnerability. The mental picture of a lion pouncing on him while his prick was in his hand was a scary one.

The noise of an engine surprised him. He glanced up and down the track. From the south, the direction they had come from, was a glow of headlights. Not the lights themselves – they must have been behind a small rise – but the extended beams, which swung left and right and up and down with the undulations of the road. The engine's roar dropped to a low growl then stopped altogether. The lights went out.

All thought of lions left Martin's mind. Alarmed, his brain cleared. This was something much closer to home. He did not know what, but Jonathan's warnings of being followed surfaced. He ran back to the cars and clambered up Jonathan's ladder. 'Gudrun, Jonathan, wake up!'

'What?'

'Wake up! There's a vehicle stopped down the road. They may be hunters, I dunno, but if we're being followed …?'

The benefit of past experience showed. 'We've got to get out of here. We'll go on foot. Bring water and your hat.' Jonathan scrambled into his clothes, clashing with Gudrun in the limited space. She hadn't said anything; the course of action was obvious to her.

Outside, Martin was still pulling on a shirt and ramming his hat on his head. 'Come on, Ginny, come on.'

'Have you got your water?'

'Yes. Come on!'

'Bring your car keys.' Jonathan wasn't sure why he said that, but having the keys could come in handy later and might, just might, at least deny anyone else their vehicles.

He led them away into the bush, Gudrun bringing up the rear. Jonathan set a fast pace; there was enough light to see the way between the widely spaced little trees. He walked away from the track for ten minutes, then turned south in a direction he hoped was parallel to it. It would take them back in the direction they had come to eventually meet the cutline.

They stopped to rest after forty minutes. Ginny said, 'Isn't this taking us towards those people?'

'Yes, which is the last thing they'll expect. Hopefully, if they're after us, they're right next to the road and will already be at our camp. A touch of déjà vu, lover?'

Gudrun shook her head. 'I can't believe we're going through this again.'

21

Unlike that time in Mozambique, the night sky was clear, with millions more stars than they were used to seeing. Ginny identified the Southern Cross.

Gudrun said, 'Sometimes we have clear nights like this at home and we see as many stars, maybe more. But I don't recognise this southern sky. Do we head straight towards the cross?'

'No, you take a line down its centre, no matter which way up it is, extend it four and a half times and directly below that is due south.'

Martin stared at Ginny in the dim light. 'How do you know that?'

'I'm a warehouse of knowledge. I thought that's why you love me. Or,' she added, 'you can bisect those two bright stars, they're called the pointers, and where that line intersects the line through the cross is the South Celestial Pole – same place.'

'Huh.'

'What do we do now?'

'It's a toss-up,' Jonathan said. 'We can carry on until we hit the cutline and then on to the main road, but that's a long way from here. It'll be tough to do with limited water. As an alternative, we can go back to our cars. If we go to the cutline those people will find us, because it's the logical thing for us to do. But if we go to the cars, they might be waiting in case we return.'

After a few minutes while everyone considered the options, Jonathan said, 'I'm in favour of going back to the cars once it gets light.'

'Or …' said Gudrun. 'We could go straight back towards the track and try to see where these people are and what they're doing. We must be beyond where Martin saw them stop, so if we turn back to our vehicles and they've gone, we can carry on. I think it's the best way to approach our camp.'

Jonathan put it to the vote and put up his finger, but Martin hesitated on seeing Ginny had not moved. She raised her hand, not to vote but to silence them. 'Shhh! Listen.'

'What?'

'Shhh!'

The distant sound of an engine came to them from the direction of the road. There was a brief glimpse of headlights flashing up at the sky and pointing back towards the cutline. They listened to the noise wavering as the car encountered sticky patches in the sand.

'They've gone, we can go straight back now,' Martin said.

Jonathan took a sip of water. 'I think we should follow Gudrun's idea anyway. Suppose they left a couple of men to wait for us to return? What if we aim for the cars and miss them because we went too far north? No, going to the track will ensure we don't get lost at least, and we should approach our Landies very carefully.'

'Now?' said Ginny.

'No, let's wait until it's almost light. It won't be long, about an hour.'

Jonathan found Hunter's Road easily enough, so they retreated back into the bush and walked parallel to it until they saw the pan. He and Gudrun made a cautious circuit around the camp, keeping about forty metres from the Land Rovers. Sometimes the cars were in sight, sometimes hidden. If watchers were there, they would have to be a similar distance away in order to see the group arrive. The pair found nothing and declared the camp clear.

'We've a problem.' Ginny pointed to the wheels. All the tyres had been slashed, and both cars were sitting on the rims.

'Fuck!' Jonathan blurted. 'Sorry, Ginny. They think they've trapped us here, so they'll be coming back.'

'But they didn't cut these.' Gudrun was inspecting the spare wheels. 'We have two spares each, we can make one car go.'

'Okay. There's no time to waste. Martin, you and I will change the wheels on my car, using all four spares. Gudrun, Ginny, please get all the valuables from your car into ours and unload all the unnecessary stuff. We need to take six of the flat wheels to get them fixed, then we can return and recover the other vehicle and still have one spare each.'

Martin blew his nose. 'Why not forget about it? Günter said he would help with anything we needed in an emergency.'

'Because only one person knew where we were going, and that was Günter Mueller. He must have told Poh what our plans were, which is why they knew where to look for us. If we call Günter now, we'll be telling Poh what we intend to do.'

'Not if we tell him something different to our real intention,' Ginny said.

Martin was scratching a spot where something had bitten him. 'It wasn't only Günter, there was that friendly helper of his – Moses.'

'True,' Jonathan said, 'but we don't know who to trust, so unless we plant a false scent we need to keep it to ourselves.'

'It wasn't Günter Mueller.' Gudrun was emphatic.

'How can you be so certain?' said Ginny.

'The same way I knew Jonathan was the man I wanted to be with forever. I knew that within five minutes. I am certain Günter is honest. Anyway, we have time to think about it – there's no phone signal here and no way to contact him until we reach the main road.'

With the Land Rover loaded, four of the slashed wheels fastened to the roof rack, one on the bonnet and one on the back-door support, Jonathan turned north on the track.

'Aren't you going to the cutline?'

'When they come back, we'll meet them head-on if we go that way. There are other routes to the A33 further on.'

They made good progress for an hour, before reaching an open area with long grass and few bushes. It was a flood plain with what looked like black cotton soil. In the wet, elephants had walked there and left ankle-deep footprints. The earth had dried rock-hard, and this severely rutted surface slowed the Land Rover to less than walking pace as Jonathan had to bump into and out of each footprint, throwing everyone in the car from side to side.

'Stop please, I'm getting out to walk over this stuff, it's horrible,' Gudrun complained.

'Me too,' Ginny agreed.

Martin laughed. 'And me. You're on your own, Jonathan.'

The vehicle was about half way across the elephant tracks when the walkers heard the noise, turned back and saw the Cessna coming towards them. The pilot was flying low this time, only at a couple of hundred feet, and making no attempt to hide his interest.

Jonathan had not been aware of the aircraft – he was facing

away from it and the noise of his own engine covered its approach. The sudden roar from above was startling. He pressed on. He saw where the elephants had left the track a little further ahead and looked forward to the freedom of movement once he reached the end of this body-twisting ride. He watched the Cessna climb away. *What's he going to do now? Poh, if it's him, has identified us and knows where we're going.*

Outside, the walkers had stopped to watch the machine as it gained altitude and turned right.

'He's going into Zimbabwe.' Gudrun stared after it. 'I bet it's something to do with poaching, and I bet Poh's involved.'

'What do you suppose he's doing there?'

Martin saw the little aircraft had not gained much height after its initial climb. 'Whatever he's doing, it's illegal. You're not allowed to fly over game reserves below about fifteen hundred feet, and he's certainly not that high.'

Jonathan had stopped under some trees after the point where the track became smooth again. He waited for the group to join him.

'What do you think?' Ginny was still staring at the diminishing dot in the sky.

'Whoever tried to get to us last night would have returned this morning thinking we were stranded and we would take the shortest route back to the main road on foot. They must have found we'd left and now he's traced us; the aircraft will tell the men on the ground where we are. They won't be able to catch us on this road, so they'll try to cut us off further ahead. Let's have a look at the map.'

'I'll get some breakfast and coffee ready while you're doing that. Fifteen minutes delay is not going to hurt, and we've had nothing today.'

'Good idea Ginny, thanks.'

Martin unfolded the map and spread it out on the flat area over the front wheel. 'We're about here,' he said, identifying the flood plain.

'Agreed. There's a track to the left through a village in this forest reserve and the cutline further north. Both lead back to the A33. It's a gamble as to which one to take.'

Gudrun reached over Martin's shoulder and pointed. 'Look. Just before the next cutline is an area which could be thick vegetation. We could hide in there until it gets dark, then drive the cutline back to civilisation tonight.'

'Bloody good idea. But a little further, beyond the cutline, is an area of even denser bush. If we went there and they saw us, they would think we were going to carry on along this road. Let's do that. Once it's dark we'll turn back for the cutline. It can't be difficult, and better to tackle it at night than some indistinct track.'

'Breakfast's up, such as it is.'

As they helped themselves to Ginny's limited offering, there was the clear, but distant, sound of an automatic rifle.

Jonathan frowned and studied Martin and Ginny's reaction. They glanced at each other first, and then at him, alarm and uncertainty on their faces.

To Gudrun and I, though, the sound of gunfire regurgitates our first-hand experience of sickening slaughter. The repercussions are ominous, and I'll have to watch her.

'That came from the Zim side, the game reserve. You don't shoot animals in a reserve with an automatic weapon unless you're a poacher.' Gudrun's words were snapped out, releasing some of her suppressed anger. Ginny stared at her in surprise.

'It came from the direction the Cessna took,' Jonathan said. 'I've had another thought. After that flypast I think it's going to be difficult hiding this vehicle from anyone above. The aircraft is going to come back past us on its way home, or come out later to find out where we'll be tonight. We should turn onto the next cutline and start heading towards the main road so it sees what we're doing. When it's gone, we'll turn back and continue on Hunter's Road to Kasane and drive all night if necessary. With a bit of luck, Poh and co will lay a trap for us on the cutline or aim to intercept us on the A33. When we don't appear, they'll come looking in the morning, by which time we'll be getting our tyres repaired.'

There was universal agreement on that idea. They had plenty of time to reach the turn-off before late afternoon, so they continued the drive at leisure. The Cessna passed overhead on its way back west in the late morning. Two hours before sunset, it flew back into Zimbabwe, giving no indication it had seen the Land Rover.

By that time, the group had passed the track which led to the village and were approaching the cutline. When they reached it, Jonathan turned left onto the wide cleared strip before stopping to let everyone out to stretch their legs.

<h1 style="text-align:center">22</h1>

First impressions of silence in the bush were an illusion. Outside the car, a light northerly breeze whispered in their ears, birds called and, if the group listened, the rustle of unseen movement could be heard. The occasional mechanical tick of the Land Rover's cooling engine added a harsh, foreign sound. Above these innocent noises penetrated the distant drone of the Cessna. It was coming from deeper in Zimbabwe and heading straight towards them. The engine note lowered and they saw the little aeroplane descending, still on course for the cutline where they stood.

'I don't like this.' Martin was staring at the approaching aircraft. 'Do you think he's going to attack us?'

Jonathan laughed. 'Don't be daft. What's he going to do, light a fuse and drop a little bomb as they did in World War One?'

'He could use a grenade.'

'A bit hit and miss. No, he's just going to make sure we know he's still watching us.'

'I wish I had a rifle,' Gudrun said. 'I'm tired of this man.'

'Hang on, he's not coming here, he's turning south. He's

getting low.'

Ginny rejoined them from taking a break behind some bushes. 'What's happening?'

'Now he's turning north. His flaps are down, he's landing!' Jonathan said. 'There must be an airstrip behind those trees.'

Gudrun thumped her fist into her other palm. 'We've got to see what's going on.'

Her intense expression caused his earlier worries about her attitude to resurface. He inclined his head towards the other two. 'Yes, but—'

'No buts, Jonathan. This is a chance to get real evidence against someone. You heard the shots. An animal was killed. This aircraft has been watching us, and we were attacked. Now he's landing after a kill. That only means one thing – Poh, or whoever, is going to take the horn or trophy away. We've got to see that. We have to photograph it. Come on!'

'You're right. Martin, you two stay here. I won't have you involved in this.'

'No way, I'm coming with you.'

'For God's sake, hurry up,' said Gudrun. 'We'll never get evidence if you two stand here arguing.'

Martin had the expression of a dog whose owners were leaving him alone at home.

'Martin, please. Don't be stupid. Think of Ginny being in danger. I'm not letting Gudrun go alone, but any more than two would increase the chance of being seen. Besides, it's vital for us to have you safe away from the action and able to go and get help if it all goes wrong.'

Ginny interrupted. 'Jonathan's right, my love, it's better this way.'

'I'm always in support, never directly involved.'

'This is not a prank, this is serious, and your support is vital, Martin. It always has been – please.'

'*Come on.* I'll go on my own if you don't hurry.'

Jonathan stifled his reply. The frustration in her voice was rising. She was not interested in their argument, only focused on getting to see the handover of a rhino horn. But she'd have to wait until he sorted his friend out. 'Martin, when you hear the aircraft start up again, take the Land Rover and drive along the cutline so he sees you as he goes home. When he's gone, turn back and wait here. We'll meet you as soon as we can.' He turned and ran after Gudrun, who had given up waiting and was rushing away.

Together they half-ran, half-walked towards the noise of the Cessna's engine.

'He's still taxiing, we've got time,' Jonathan panted.

'We'd have a lot more time if you didn't waste it in a stupid argument. That delay talking to Martin might have cost us the evidence that has to be there.'

Jonathan clenched his teeth, but said nothing.

'Why do you have to explain everything to Martin the way you do? You treat him like your puppy. He's an adult, he doesn't need your protection.'

'I don't treat him like a puppy. He's been a tremendous support for me several times, invaluable, and he's a good friend. I look after his best interests because he'll put himself in situations where he would be out of his depth just to support me.'

They continued in silence and, as they closed in on the place where the aircraft had to be, Gudrun took Jonathan's hand and squeezed it. They were a team, she seemed to be saying. But he was still fretting at her anger, perplexed at how she could dismiss this conflict to a separate compartment in her mind and carry on as normal. His emotions would not allow him to return the sentiment in her grasp.

Ahead of them, the engine noise died. Voices could be heard. They were close, but could see nothing, and crept forward. Gudrun put a hand out to stop him. 'I caught a glimpse of some white through there. It must be the plane,' she said, and removed her hat.

'Put that back on. You need to break up the outline of your head.'

Bent over into a crouch, they took slow step by slow step, glancing down to make sure they didn't crack any twigs. The edge of the bush was a few metres ahead of them, and the open space of a rudimentary runway stretched to the south. It was narrow and part of an existing vehicle track. *That disguises it as a runway from the air. It would be too much trouble to cut this bush back from the track for a single flight, so it must be a regular pick-up point for trophies. I wonder if the authorities know of it.*

Gudrun tugged him over to the right where the bush was thicker. He unslung his camera and adjusted the lens to maximum zoom. Keeping back behind the leaves, he built their photographic evidence.

Two scruffy men were holding a rhino horn each. Their assault rifles lay on the ground behind the aircraft. A third man was having an animated conversation with Poh via another, who was interpreting. Poh was getting angry, fidgeting with impatience to settle the deal, but the poachers just stood there, holding the horns and watching developments.

Jonathan lowered his camera for a moment. 'I think they're demanding more money.'

The head poacher spat on the ground and turned away from the argument, making some remark. The interpreter yelled back at him. Poh demanded to know what was said. There was a brief discussion between the half-Vietnamese and his translator, before Poh gave in. He counted out notes from a wad he pulled from his trouser pocket and, with a disdainful gesture, thrust them at the poacher. He barked something to the only white man in the group, who was wearing khaki trousers and a white shirt with three-bar epaulettes. The pilot handed the poachers a bag, into which they put the horns before giving it back to him. He placed it on the floor in the rear of the aircraft and nodded to them. In a manner which reeked of insolence, they sauntered towards the spot where they had left their weapons.

Neither Poh nor his interpreter made any move to leave. The situation had come to a standstill. Jonathan and Gudrun gave each other questioning glances. He shrugged and gave a slight shake of his head before turning at the sound of another engine. A battered white pickup truck was approaching down the runway belching oily blue smoke from its exhaust. It stopped at the tail of the aircraft. Poh climbed into the front, the door squeaking as he slammed it shut. The interpreter and the poachers clambered over the sides and into the load bed. Its engine stuttering what might well have been its last breath, the pickup bounced off down the runway on lively springs and worn shock absorbers. The pilot was left to guard his Cessna.

Jonathan tugged at Gudrun's sleeve, and they crept back into the bush. 'Where the hell's he going?' she said. 'This is a game reserve, you can't drive anywhere you want.'

'They don't follow the rules. Maybe the poachers have a camp set up somewhere. We need to steal the aircraft and take the horns away.'

Gudrun's eyes glinted at the prospect of positive action. 'Okay, good. You have a plan?'

'Yes, but we need the other two. Let's get back to the car. We've got to do it before Poh comes back.'

Breathless from the run, they reached the Land Rover in less than five minutes.

'Martin, Ginny, listen carefully, please.' Jonathan explained what they had seen. 'We're going to pinch the aircraft, complete with the horns, but it needs all of us to do it. You two should steal it after Gudrun and I have disabled the pilot.'

Gudrun frowned with disappointment. Ginny's suspicion was plain, but Martin almost exploded with enthusiasm. 'But don't you want to fly it?' he said, clearly hoping for the opposite.

'No. The danger will be here on the ground, not in the air, and Gudrun and I are better equipped to handle it than you two. We'll take care of the pilot, and you bugger off down the runway and away into Botswana. There's hardly any wind so the take-off direction is not important. There must be a good hour's fuel left in the machine, which means you can hold to the east of here. We need them to think you've gone far away. As soon as we've dealt with the pilot, we'll drive up the cutline to find a long enough stretch of smooth ground for you to land.'

'Okay, sounds good.' Martin glanced at Ginny, who was still sceptical, but agreed anyway.

'There might be a few problems. It's sure to be dark before we find a safe place for you to land – but remember what your dad was telling us about how it's been done before with the car's headlights?'

'Yes, but we should go through it again.'

'We will, on our way back there. Next, you need to face the fact that your landing may end up as a crash. Sorry, but the surface might be too rough. You should put out all the anchors to stop as quick as you can, because I don't know how much runway we can get for you. Short-field landing, Martin – are you sure you want to do this?'

'Damn right I do. Ginny, d'you want to come with me or stay with them?'

'I think you're daft, but I'll stick with you. Someone needs to maintain a level of common sense around here.'

'Bring one of those spare cargo straps with you.'

'What for?'

The shadows were lengthening. Already the sun was behind the treetops. Thinking he had complete privacy, the pilot was playing cowboys beside his aircraft. He was practising quick draws from the holster at his right hip, swinging round in a crouch, aiming his pistol at imaginary targets in the bush and making *pow, pow* sounds. It would have been funny at any other time, but the sight of the drawn weapon made the group hesitate.

Jonathan held his hand out to stop the others. 'I hoped he'd be resting.'

'I'll go and ask him for help,' Gudrun said. 'I'll distract him and keep him focused on me, so you can get behind him.'

Ginny shook her head. 'No, you're too intimidating. You're a head above him. You'll make him feel threatened, and in any case, Poh might have told his men to look out for the tall woman. I'll do it.'

'Okay. That makes sense.'

'Martin, stay back, we need you to be in one piece to fly the aircraft. Gudrun and I will take care of him,' said Jonathan.

Ginny walked forward towards the edge of the bush, waited until the pilot had holstered his gun one more time, and ran out towards him, crying, 'Help! Help me, please. There's been an accident. Our Toyota rolled and my husband's hurt. We've got to get the car off him. He needs a doctor. Please help!'

The other three were close enough to see clearly. The pilot's hand dropped to the butt of his gun, but he didn't draw it. He gaped at the wild, red-haired woman who had rushed out of the bush, apparently from nowhere. She went right up to him. He backed away, doubt and suspicion on his face.

'Please,' Ginny whined, 'he needs a doctor. It's terrible, the car's upside down and he's trapped. Please come and help, or get on your radio – just do something.'

She moved to his side, and he turned to continue facing her.

He had a Staffordshire accent and a tanned face. 'Who the hell are you? What're you doing? You're not allowed here.'

Ginny grabbed his hand and tugged at him. 'Come! Please!'

He shook her off and turned to keep facing her as she moved around him. 'I can't help you now. You'll have to wait until the boss comes back.'

Still under cover, Jonathan and Gudrun had crept round until the aircraft shielded them from the pilot.

The pitch of Ginny's voice was rising. 'My hubby's going to die! Please, you've got to help, please. I beg you.'

'I said I can't, now shut up and wait.' He pushed Ginny away.

Jonathan was on the far side of the Cessna. He saw the pilot's back and Ginny's desperate face. She only had to hold the man's attention for a few seconds more.

'Can't you use your radio and call for help?' she pleaded.

'It won't be able to pick up another station from the ground here. I'd have to be airborne. Now shut up and wait, will you.' He turned away from her. Another few degrees, and he would see too much.

'Can't you call another aeroplane and relay a message, or something?' Ginny reached for his hand again, drawing his attention.

Jonathan clamped his arm round the pilot's neck. He dragged the man backwards off balance. Gudrun hit him hard in the kidneys and whipped the gun out of its holster. His mouth was open. She rammed the barrel between his lips, chipping a tooth.

'*Aagh.*' His cry of pain was muffled by the gun. Expressions of fear and fury crossed his face.

Martin ran up and clambered into the aircraft. 'C'mon, Ginny, let's go,' he shouted.

She was fastening her seat belt when Martin switched on. The engine was still warm and fired at the first turn. Martin signalled with his fingers to Jonathan: 1.5 hours. He opened the throttle.

Gudrun was now holding the gun to the pilot's temple as Jonathan forced him to lie face down on the ground. He bent his right leg over into the crook of his left knee and pulled the left foot up so the right leg was trapped. The cargo strap had a buckle on the end. Jonathan made a loop and tightened it round the left foot. He wound the end twice round the pilot's neck and tied his hands together behind his back with the remainder. 'Don't struggle, or the strap will tighten round your throat.'

Martin opened the throttle wide. The little Cessna was accelerating down the runway.

Jonathan rolled the pilot onto his side so he could look him in the face. 'Quick: when is Poh getting back here?'

'Fuck off.' The words were hoarse. The strap was pressing into his larynx.

'We will, but you had better hope he gets to you before any animals sniff you out. We wouldn't want you to be eaten alive …'

'I do …' said Gudrun. She was bent down, her face a few inches from the man, her cold stare emphasising her words.

'… although we might be able to make sure that doesn't happen. How long have you got?'

'He should be back already. We have to take off before dark.'

'Then we'll leave you safe and sound. We'll let the police know the registration of your aircraft – you should expect a few questions.'

'Bye-ee!' Gudrun gave him an evil grin.

They ran and reached the bush. A loud thump came from down the runway. Jonathan stopped and looked back. The pickup was visible, weaving around before stopping, but the Cessna was out of sight, low down behind the trees.

'Bloody hell, I hope we can pull this off. We don't need anyone injured. There's no way the aircraft can land on this stuff without ending up in a heap.'

The Land Rover was covering rough ground as Jonathan drove along the cutline, the going slow. Gudrun had braced herself, pushing back into the seat and clinging on to the dash for stability. They were heading into the setting sun, most of which had already vanished below the horizon, leaving a brilliant orange segment and a gorgeous red glow across the sky, with not a cloud in sight. It was beautiful and bright enough to cast the detail of the surface they needed to assess into deep shadow. The end of the day had reached that difficult stage when it was neither truly dark, nor light enough to see detail. Outside the car, the temperature had dropped.

After about a kilometre the ride became smoother. Jonathan noted the odometer reading. '45.2. Remember that, and we'll see if we can get more than a flat three hundred metres.'

The going stayed good until they reached another area of deep elephant footprints. Jonathan checked the odometer again. 'It's just turning to 45.5. That's not enough, I'm sure it's not enough. I would need to see the performance charts to be certain, but they're landing on a dirt runway with a slight tailwind at about three thousand feet altitude. I think it'll need more than three hundred metres to stop from where he passes over us. Hell!'

Gudrun touched his arm. 'We could search for another ten kilometres and find nothing better. If what you say is correct, they will have slowed right down by the time they hit this area. If they run into these holes, what danger is it to them at slow speed? Also, time is not on our side, we don't know what Poh is doing.'

'You're right. The plane is going to be buggered, but that's not our concern. They shouldn't suffer more than a bruise or two – unless it catches fire. We'll have to risk it. I don't want to play with other people's lives, though. We need to mark the end of our runway.'

Gudrun got out and put a camping light on the ground in the centre of the track. It had a flashing feature which she found after some fiddling, and switched it on. She rose from her crouch and turned around, then rushed back to the Land Rover. 'My God! Look *Sæti*, look!'

Silhouetted against the red and orange sunset was the unmistakeable shape of an elephant, then another, and another. Great black hulks swaying as they moved along the cutline; a whole herd of them. The odd one deviated and snatched branches off a tree to the side, but the march continued, an unrelenting mass moving towards them with deceptive speed.

'We'd better get out of the way, they're only about a hundred metres off.' Jonathan turned the car around and drove away, staying well ahead of the herd, but keeping them in sight. 'They're going to be a problem if they stay on the cutline, we won't be able to get Martin to land.'

'And we don't know what Poh's doing,' Gudrun repeated. 'He might be after us.'

'In that clapped-out truck?

'It's becoming really difficult to see the elephants.'

'I'll stop and switch off. Let's get out and see if we can hear them. Don't make a noise, although they must know we're here.'

Each by their door, they peered into a sky which had

turned a dark blue. Stars were glittering in the east and becoming more visible to the west. Of the elephants they heard nothing at first, then the crack of a branch sounded nearby. A deep stomach rumble was close. In the background was the faint sound of a lonely little aeroplane.

'They're not far, *Sœti*, I think we should move.' Gudrun whispered. For once there was a hint of nervousness in her voice.

'There's one right here! We need to go. Now!'

He started the engine and put some distance between them and the herd before slowing down again.

'Any moment and we'll be at the rough bit again and won't be able to travel fast enough. We need to get off this track and let them pass. I'm going to try. You'd better pray we don't get stuck.'

The rumble had come from the middle of the track; the breaking branch had been to their left. Jonathan chose the opposite direction. Worried that the brilliance of the headlights would disturb the elephants, he put on the sidelights, and they strained to see the ditch by the track and the little trees which blocked their way. Somehow he managed to get the car around, off the track but facing it. He switched off the engine and doused the lights. They could only sit and wait.

'Damn this. We need to get moving.'

'My God!' Gudrun put her hand out and clutched Jonathan's. A massive dark hulk was only a few feet in front of the car, moving past without turning its head. It paused. There was another splintering and crackle of wood being ripped. The shape ambled on without further sound, and disappeared into the dark.

Her hand still holding Jonathan's, Gudrun squeezed hard. 'They know we're here, they couldn't care. That was wonderful, just fantastic!'

'I wonder if they've all gone? … Look, those lights through there, at the end of the cutline!'

'It must be Poh.'

'Shit! That's stuffed Martin's landing, even if the elephants don't.'

The headlights swung to face up the cutline and moved forward. They stopped, and a figure emerged out of the dark to walk in front of them.

'He's looking for a route over the rough ground,' Jonathan said. 'I don't think the vehicle will be able to cross that surface, he'll bottom out because some of the holes are so deep.'

They heard the sound of the pickup's engine revving. The man in front kept moving in and out of the headlights, scouting the way.

As they watched, the lights flickered, shuttered into an indecipherable Morse code by thick striding legs as the elephants passed in front of them. The engine note rose to a roar as the driver panicked to reverse. An elephant vented its anger, trumpeting a great scream at the sound of the vehicle's spinning wheels as it crashed over the bumps.

'Now's our chance!' Jonathan put on the headlights and moved back onto the cutline before switching them off again. Poh should not be given any opportunity to see where they were, but the pickup seemed to have escaped.

It wasn't long before they found the place where the smooth part of the track began and Jonathan turned the car around to line it up with the makeshift runway.

'The idea is to use the hazard lights to show Martin where we are. When we hear he's close, I'll switch on the extra driving lights on the roof rack and put the headlights on full beam in the direction of landing. With those and his landing lights, Martin should be able to cope – I hope, anyway. All he's got to do is come in low, right over the top of us, aiming for the light you set up at the other end of the runway. As soon as he's touched down he needs to slam on the brakes and skid his way to a stop before he ends up in a heap. That's the theory, anyway. Neither of us has done this before, and Martin is not a natural pilot, sad to say.'

'So why are you letting him do this? Now you're the one putting your friend in danger.'

'Two reasons. He's desperate to take a more positive role instead of just being in support. I need to let him see I recognise that. And secondly, being on the ground here having to face Poh could be much more dangerous than the landing.'

23

Having started the aircraft engine, Martin had not looked back to see how Jonathan and Gudrun were dealing with the pilot. There was no time to waste, Poh could return at any moment. He lined the aircraft up at the end of the rudimentary airstrip. A quick check to see the engine temperatures were in their green arcs, and he opened the throttle.

'The pickup! It's going to cut us off!' Ginny shouted. She scrabbled for something to hold on to.

Martin did not reply. Utterly focused on the take off, he was willing the airspeed to rise. *Come on, come on …* But it climbed at less than its normal rate, because they were not on a hard surface. He pushed the throttle again, but it was full open. The pickup was turning onto the runway to face the oncoming aircraft. Martin's mind raced over the figures. *We're at around three thousand feet here and the temperature is higher than at home. It's going to take more runway to get airborne, much more, and bloody Poh is aiming straight at us.* He kept switching his glance from the runway to the airspeed indicator and back to the runway and the fast-approaching truck.

The men in the back of the vehicle had a fleeting impact on Martin's attention. Clutching the rail at the front of the load bed, their heads were above the cab. They looked alarmed. They meant nothing to him. His entire focus was on getting the little Cessna airborne. Leaning forward, tense with concentration, he willed the machine to accelerate. *42 knots, it's too slow. We'll stall. Come on!*

Ginny's bottom lip was clenched between her teeth. She flicked a worried glance at Martin. 'He's going to ram us!'

47 knots, can I chance it? 50.

'Martin, do something!'

One of those mental snapshots of great clarity which etch themselves in one's memory forever: bang in front of him, Poh screaming at the driver. The driver, his eyes bulging, his forearm rising to shield his face, and his mouth set in a hideous gape. The men in the load bed ducking down, one with his hand on his head.

If they weren't fast enough, it would be too late. Martin had to get over the truck. He pulled back, praying they wouldn't stall. The Cessna leapt into the air. *Not too much! We'll lose airspeed and crash.*

A hideous thump. The left wheel hit the top of the pickup's cab. The aircraft slewed and lurched, the hesitation costing vital knots. A brief quiver ran through the machine as the undercarriage vibrated with the blow.

Instead of predictable tension, an unexpected calm settled on him, enabling him to think and act with precision. He eased the nose down to regain lost airspeed. The ground loomed. He drew back on the control column. The Cessna flew level with the surface, skimming it, while accelerating knot by gradual knot. Martin, without saying a word, settled into the climb before turning west.

Once he'd established that everything was normal, he sat

back. *'Whew!'* He glanced across at Ginny. 'Close enough for you?'

'Martin, have you ever heard me swear?'

'No, never.'

'Bloody, fucking hell!' she screamed.

He burst out laughing.

They set course into the setting sun. Ginny had flown with her man before and knew how to work the GPS. She set the Hunter's Road and cutline intersection as a waypoint so they could find their way back in the dark.

About five miles to the east, three thousand feet above the ground and where he hoped they were out of earshot from Poh, Martin established a racetrack pattern to hold and wait. He throttled back to the most economical settings and tried to think of everything which could affect a safe landing onto a bush road: an unknown surface, in the dark, using only car headlights. For over thirty minutes they circled, keeping a constant lookout for the Land Rover's hazard lights.

'I hope I didn't damage that wheel or the leg. It might fail on landing. And another thing: the fuel level's dropping. We've about forty minutes left.'

'You're a real morale-raiser, aren't you? What are we going to do when it's too low to carry on?'

'The only thing we can do is head for the main road to land. We should see it from the vehicle lights. There's not much traffic – I'm sure we'll be able to find a gap between the trucks to touch down.'

'This is madness. You and Jonathan are crazy, and I'm stupid enough to follow you. Hey! I thought I saw lights, but not hazards. Yes, there they are again. See, Martin?'

'Got 'em. I'm going closer. They've gone – what now?'

Two minutes passed.

'There's Jonathan, his hazards are flashing.'

'I see them, and I can also see the light at the runway end –

it's pretty dim. It looks bloody short!'

'Martin, tell me the good news, will you?'

Martin turned wide and, keeping the hazards in sight, manoeuvred the machine to get them and the light at the runway's end lined up. It was difficult, because there was no perspective in all the blackness, which meant he could not tell distance nor see their height. All he could do was use the lights for direction and make a gradual descent to some fifty feet above the altitude they had taken off from. He hoped to be almost over the Land Rover at that point. But all the time he had the feeling they were descending into a black hole ending in the ground. An amateur, all he could rely on were his altimeter and a vague idea of the size of the vehicle in his mind; he had no experience to fall back on. Terry, his dad, the airline captain who had taught both him and Jonathan to fly, was not going to be amused when he relayed the story; if they survived, that was.

'Put your headlights on, Jonathan. Put them on, please, it's time,' Martin muttered to himself. He glanced at Ginny. 'This is going to be a short field landing. That means we come in steep and slow, and the touchdown may be pretty solid. We'll pass the car on my side. I'll try not to hit it. I'll brake hard, but this is a dirt runway and it will take time to stop. We may skid, and I'm worried about the undercarriage leg. Here's hoping it holds.'

As if on cue, the Land Rover headlights came on followed by the roof-mounted array to light the track. Martin now had a better picture to work with, and was well positioned. He had been prepared to go around and have another attempt if it appeared too bad the first time, but this looked good. At least, it did at first.

'Lock your harness, Ginny love.' He selected full flaps. The little aeroplane's nose dropped, and the immediate brake on the speed pressed them forward in their seats. Martin adjusted the power. Beside him, he sensed Ginny's tension rising as if it were his own. He worried for her. She might be injured, or worse. He wanted to tell her to close her eyes, to shut out the scene of the crash which was coming, but could not. She, like him, had to face it. He had to put thoughts of her behind him and concentrate. His pulse accelerated as each action he took brought the climax to this potentially disastrous event closer, step by step.

Martin aimed a little beyond the front of the car and to its right. He didn't tell Ginny, but he knew all about the 'black hole' effect, the visual illusion which causes pilots to fly too low an approach at night and end up crashing short of the airstrip. Even on a runway with lights all along its length it could happen, but on this occasion Martin only had lights at the start and the runway end – precious little guidance. His dad had drummed caution about night landings into him, and so Martin focused on keeping the approach angle high, which would avoid trouble – he hoped.

Down they came. Minutes became seconds. He kept checking the picture he had of the runway's length and focused on keeping the Land Rover's lights in the same position in the windshield. If they moved down, he was getting too high and might have to go around and try again. If they moved up, he would be getting too low and might well hit the car. He was tensing up, his muscles making stiff and excessive movements. *Relax! Take it easy, you're doing okay.* He tensed again. *Relax! Focus on the car, keep it there, in that spot …*

The roof of the Land Rover, the lights at the front of it, rushed up at them. Fine details of the surface became apparent. They were too low. The car was in the way. Martin gave a burst of power, and the left wing cleared the roof rack by inches. A fleeting glimpse of Gudrun and Jonathan's pale worried faces could not distract him.

Martin flared the Cessna and cut the throttle, slowing it. But the little burst of power had delayed the touch-down. The Cessna seemed to hang in space, grass and dirt flashing past, eating up precious runway. The speed fell and the plane settled, threatening to drop with a bang.

They thumped onto the ground, harder than normal, but they were down, racing along the track. They were slowing all the time, but it wasn't enough. The runway end light was just ahead. They were still going too fast.

'Shit! I can't stop before the end, no way. Hold on, Ginny!'

The camping lamp disappeared beneath them. A second later a crash into a hole and a shattering bang. The nose wheel collapsed, the propeller struck the ground and dug in. The aircraft tipped forward over its nose, stopping, poised in a vertical position as if undecided what to do, then flopped over onto its back. They were left hanging in their harnesses.

'You okay, Ginny? Get out now! Think fire!'

Martin couldn't open his door, it was jammed. Ginny undid her belt and dropped head down to the cockpit roof, scrabbling for a hold to gain some stability. Twisting about, she struggled to disentangle herself and get out. Martin scrambled his way across the cockpit to follow, helped her up and ran her away from the wreck.

Jonathan had chased the Cessna down the runway. The Land Rover was there now, headlights on the scene. He switched them off and went to join the others.

'Well done my friend, that was a perfect touchdown, considering ...'

'One of my better ones, actually.' Martin laughed in relief. 'Not bad for a genius.'

'We need to get out of here – Poh was after us earlier, but couldn't make it this far. We don't know where he is now.

'What are you doing?' he called.

Gudrun was striding towards the wreck. 'I'm getting the horns. That's what we came for wasn't it?'

'Gudrun, NO! There are flames there!' Ginny never yelled, but she did then. 'Gudrun, FIRE! Get away from it.'

Jonathan couldn't see the flames, but now was not a time to argue. Shouting at Gudrun would have no effect whatsoever. He leapt after her, reaching the Cessna at the same time. He grabbed her arm, but she shook him free. The bag with two horns was lying by the broken rear windows.

Jonathan saw the flames now, behind the engine firewall, which had crumpled. Fuel was leaking from a split line in the windshield pillar. It would ignite any moment. The fuel tanks, on the top of the aircraft, were now on the ground, possibly punctured. Gudrun was on her stomach reaching into the back. Jonathan grabbed her feet and pulled. She gave a violent kick. He lost his grip and fell back. She lunged forward again and caught the neck of the bag. Again he seized her ankles and yanked her out of the airframe. The flames had spread across the ground and reached the fuel line. He let go of her legs and gripped her collar, hauling her to her feet and away from the wreck.

'You stupid, stupid woman! The horns are not worth your life.'

'Be quiet, Jonathan! I am alive, and we have the horns. One hundred per cent success, yes?'

God! How do I handle this woman and keep her and others safe? Is this to be my role in life?

When they were halfway to the other two, a blast of hot air hit their backs with a solid *whoomp*. They both stumbled forward with the blow. Ginny and Martin's faces were lit in orange, their arms raised as shields.

Jonathan stood looking back at the blaze and seethed. Gudrun was reckless to the point of idiocy. Before, he had worried how she disregarded the safety of others in her desire to achieve something, but this was her own life she had gambled with. But of course it had to wait. Once again, there was another, more pressing, matter to deal with.

'The next question is: what will Poh do now? Think about it while we move out of the fire's light, we're too exposed here.'

'He'll come here,' said Ginny. 'He's bound to have seen the fire and will think there's a chance he can salvage the horns.'

'Maybe. And if he hasn't realised we crashed?' Martin said. 'He'll think we flew a long way away and there's no point in his trying to get along this cutline as it's so rough.'

Jonathan thought about that. 'If he hasn't realised you crashed, I agree. I think he'll head north on Hunter's Road, which is quite smooth, to Pandamatenga. There's a border post there and only a short stretch of tarred road to the A33, from where he can get a mobile signal to call in his bully-boys. If he thinks we escaped on this cutline, he'll also reckon his men will catch us where it meets the main road.'

'The worst case,' Gudrun said, 'is the one we should deal with. He will have seen the plane coming in to land, he would be intent on catching us all, so he would want to come here anyway. When he heard the crash or sees the fire he would expect to find injured people, which would slow us down. He will come – soon – and we must be prepared.'

'Exactly.'

'Yes, but what do we do Ginny?' Jonathan said. 'Remember, he's armed. If we drive on to get out of his way we could meet his bruisers at the main road. We can't go back to Hunter's Road without driving past him.'

Using both hands, Jonathan dusted soil off his trousers while they considered their next move.

'I've got it,' he said. 'Martin and Ginny, you take the Land Rover and continue along the cutline for a while; not too far, so we'll still be able to reach you. Gudrun and I will wait here to see what Poh does if he comes. Another thing – I think he'll come on foot. The pickup is either going to get stuck on the rough ground, or will be so slow that it'll be quicker for him to walk it. Which means we won't know when he's coming until he's here. Let's go.'

Martin didn't argue or appear disappointed with his role this time. He was obviously feeling satisfied with himself for pulling off an extremely difficult and dangerous landing, and was content to do as requested.

They all ran for the Land Rover and made a lot of noise in driving it around the fire to the darkness on the far side. Gudrun and Jonathan got out of the car, leaving Martin to drive on, negotiating the bumps and holes one by one.

They found a spot out of the fire's light and lay down. The flames were dying anyway as the limited amount of fuel left in the Cessna was consumed. They waited, and waited.

They spoke in whispers. 'Surely he should be here by now, if he's coming?'

'You would think so. Let's give it another fifteen minutes. It's been over half an hour since the crash. He could walk here in that time.'

The fifteen minutes passed in silence, so they waited fifteen more.

Gudrun's hand searched for his. It was warm, but he could not bring himself to respond to her touch with his normal gentle stroking, which, she admitted, always sent tingles up her arm. She was watching him in the dim glow of the dying fire, and he knew she was trying to read his face. When she released his hand, an incredible sadness enveloped him. It settled in his soul, moulding him into a different person. For a few moments he lay still, his eyes closed.

'He's not coming,' he said at last. 'He's had plenty of time to get here. We need to join Martin – we have to get moving if we want to reach Kasane before dawn.'

As they stumbled over the rough ground to find the Land Rover, Jonathan could only mumble monosyllabic replies when Gudrun tried a few times to talk. Only when they found Martin and Ginny did he say more than a few words.

'Wherever Poh is, he didn't come to the wreck. He must have taken Hunter's Road to Pandamatenga.'

24

The night drive was not fun. There were too many jolts to allow them a semblance of rest, and the threat of a puncture without a spare wheel, or the possibility of a breakdown without a second vehicle in support, were worries which were amplified by their inability to communicate with the outside world.

Where the route was open, their headlights lit the track for a long way ahead, but in areas where the trees were close and the road wound its way between them, the light reflected off overhanging branches, and foliage enclosed the vehicle in its own claustrophobic tunnel.

'Sorry, I have to go slowly along these stretches,' Jonathan said. 'We know there are elephants about and if we surprise one as we pop round a tree, he'll be pissed off. We'll be scared piss-less, and there's no question who will win. We'll be far too close, with no room to turn.'

They saw more game than they had during the day, which was a positive experience: two hyenas and an aardvark made a brief appearance. Many eyes, reflected pinpoints in the headlights, gave worried stares before switching off as their owners ducked away. A wonderful but brief glimpse of a pride of lions walking down the track before they turned off gave Martin pause for thought. 'We don't have a clue, do we? You saw the elephants earlier, and we've seen their dung everywhere. There must be hundreds of them around, but we've only seen a fraction. I found that lion print yesterday, and now there was a pride in front of us. A few seconds later they move into the bush and vanish, yet they're close. We just don't know, we're so ignorant.'

In the dark, the road went on without end. Hour after hour, the engine note rose and fell with every change of gear and every variation in the surface. Nothing could be seen outside the tiny shifting world in the headlights. Now and then someone would shine a torch to the side, hoping for an exciting glimpse of wildlife.

Jonathan drove mechanically, responding to the car's demands without thinking, and remaining silent most of the time. Lack of sleep, the stress of the day's events, being on constant alert for animals and rough spots in the track, all combined to sap the strength from his mind. He wrapped himself in his own world and brooded. *Is this it? Is it over, or the end in sight? Our chalice of happiness has split. Everything I've been living for over the past year, all our dreams, our excitement about the future, is pouring from the crack. I love this woman so much, but if she can't curb her wild side then being together will not be possible. She has no concern for herself or others, and little for me. Her recklessness is driving us apart. But is it me? Is it my Dad's influence, as she suggested, his incessant preaching about safety, or have I become a weaker person, more and more cautious by the day? No, it's not me, dammit! She's in the wrong. But how do I get her to accept it?*

And now things are awkward. She tried talking to me but I could not answer, I am so close to the edge. Now, she's given up trying and is only chatting to the others. God, I'm pathetic. Tired, but still pathetic.

'What do you think Jonathan?' Gudrun peered across at him.

'Eh? Sorry, what?'

Ginny tapped his seat. 'Haven't you been listening? We were discussing what to do with the horns. If we take them to someone like a police officer or a wildlife official, how do we know we can trust them? Poh has a lot of influence.'

Martin leaned forward. 'We could bury them and pick them up later when we've found a trustworthy person. One thing's for sure, we can't leave them in the car. If they're found we'll be arrested. We've got to get rid of them. At least until we feel we're on safe ground, just in case we need them for some reason in the future.'

Gudrun had not commented on what she considered her possessions. Jonathan glanced at her. She was studying him, but because of the dark he could not see the concern on her face.

Ginny leaned forward beside Martin so their two heads were close together and almost between Jonathan and Gudrun. 'The question is, do we need them? We already have photographic evidence of Poh accepting them. And there will be a lot of explaining to do as to how we came by the horns, which will be difficult, to say the least. I think we should get rid of them – they're a liability; and we've done the main thing, which is to deprive Poh of them.'

'So what do you think, Jonathan?' Gudrun repeated.

He had been as tired as this before, more so, but never had fatigue brought on such despondency. 'Whatever.'

Jonathan pulled himself together after a short silence. 'You're right. The horns are no use to us, and it's too much of a risk to hold on to them. We don't know anyone we can trust.'

Weary, they reached the small border town of Kasane on

the Zambezi River some time after two the next morning. A quick drive around unearthed a tyre repair shop. Parking outside, they tried to get some sleep before dawn. Gudrun leaned across and kissed her man on the cheek. 'Well done, *Sœti*. You must be tired.'

He didn't answer, but rested his head on the door pillar and beckoned sleep.

He woke a bit later, shifted his position and drifted off again. Half conscious, he heard Gudrun whisper to whoever might be awake, 'I know exactly what to do with the horns.'

Silence but for a quiet snore.

'Thet not good,' agreed the large, heavy-set man who ran the tyre shop as he inspected the wheels. He scratched his balding head. 'How the hell did thet happen? Thet the kind of thing they do in the cities, not here. You make an enemy of someone, eh?'

The man, who called himself Hennie, was eager to talk. Jonathan didn't answer. Hennie shrugged his shoulders. 'Okay. Lemme check the stock, and I see what I can do for you. If I got this size, no problem, *boet*. If I haven't, you have to wait. I got another load coming. Should be here the day after tomorrow. I might be able to do an emergency repair on these two tyres and fit inner tubes, just to get you home.' He pointed. 'Those there are shot, you need new ones. You guys want some coffee? You look *baie moeg* to me. I get my wife to make it now-now.'

Jonathan went back to the others and told them the news. 'He's offered us coffee while he fixes two of them. Come on, I need a wake-up.'

Hennie's wife was a woman of mixed race. Obese, she made sluggish movements and said nothing to the visitors. She was cheery though, and joked with her husband in Afrikaans while she prepared the coffee, which was boiling to death in a pot.

'Rebecca don't speak English,' Hennie explained. 'I can see the question in your eye, so I tell you. I never agreed with apartheid down south. I came to love her, and the best place to go with her was Botswana. They friendly and relaxed here, no problem. This business is good, someone always has a tyre problem, and I can fix them good. But I never seen tyres cut on purpose before. Where this happen?'

There was no harm in talking about it, but before Jonathan could answer, Martin did. 'On Hunter's Road. We've no idea who, though.'

'Jeez! Thet's blerry odd. Thet not a place to do damage.' He shook his head for a while, thinking. 'You should report it. They won't catch 'em, but it would be a record for them to use later if there another one.'

After half an hour, they had two serviceable wheels which they mounted on the Land Rover. Jonathan asked Hennie how much it cost.

'Ag, where you go now?'

'We're going to look at the Falls, then we'll be back when your stock is in.'

'Thet job was nothing. You can pay me then, no problem.' Hennie laughed. 'Easy, eh? Just one invoice.'

'Thanks. That's good of you.'

'Take a tip. There a five-star hotel near the Falls, Zambian side. Blerry good for a drink, but too blerry expensive to stay. A little bit this way, a few k's, there a good campsite. Stay there, there always space. From the hotel, there a little walk to the end of the Falls, the Eastern Cataract. Good view, right up close to the water.'

'Thanks, Hennie. We'll see you in a couple of days.'

As they walked back to the car where Martin and Ginny were waiting, the bitter taste of boiled coffee clinging to their mouths, Gudrun sounded like a stern teacher when she said, 'Jonathan, you and I need to talk later.'

He took a deep breath. Things were coming to a head, and he was scared stiff.

25

Jonathan's original intention to be the first in the queue for the ferry across the Zambezi was thwarted by having to wait for their tyres to be repaired. By the time they had driven from Kasane to the dock at Kazungula, there was already a substantial line of vehicles ranging from big articulated lorries to motorbikes. The organisation was not straightforward, though, as the load was selected to come forward according to what mix would fit on the vessel. This would be anything from several cars to a single truck plus two or three smaller vehicles. Jonathan was directed to slot in behind a huge pantechnicon, as was a white Nissan Patrol.

The ferries were basic – flat pontoons with one ramp at either end for access which was lifted before each crossing. A bridge with the helmsman was set high on a pylon clear of the deck, and two big diesel engines, one on each side, were set outboard of the load space to drive the propellers.

The crossing was a little over half a kilometre. They all got out of the Land Rover to stretch their legs, stand at the rail and watch the mighty river passing beneath them.

Martin pulled at Jonathan's sleeve and indicated with his

head to the side. 'Come over here for a moment, will you.'

Separated from the girls, Jonathan raised his eyebrows in a silent question.

Martin prodded his friend in the chest. 'What's the matter with you?'

'I'm tired. Sorry if I'm grumpy.'

'We're all tired, especially you, but there's more to it than that. Ginny is questioning it, and she's asked Gudrun, but she doesn't know what's eating you either. There's something wrong. Come on, you can tell me. You know that.'

It was not in Jonathan's nature to talk about personal matters to anyone, even Martin.

'I'm feeling exhausted.' He stared out over the water.

'Rubbish. You need to talk it out.'

Jonathan turned away from his friend and walked back to the women.

Gudrun was uneasy. 'I have a distinct feeling of being watched, that we're not alone. I don't like it.'

Ginny agreed. 'I feel the same. It's not good.'

Martin laughed. 'The problem with Gudrun is she believes in elves. Any funny feelings and the elves are scurrying around her and causing trouble.'

'Oh, be quiet you ignorant little man! Just because I was scared in the forest when Barry Castle was stalking me and I thought of elves does not mean I believe in them, it means my childhood fears were aroused, that's all.'

'You should listen to us women, Martin. If we both say we're being watched, we are.'

Gudrun looked to see what Jonathan's reaction was, but he wasn't paying attention. He was trying to see who was in the Nissan, but, like many vehicles there, it had tinted windows and the occupants stayed in the car. *I wish he'd snap out of his sullen mood. What on earth is troubling him?*

The other ferry was approaching them from the Zambian bank – they departed at the same time, so would cross midstream. It was time. Gudrun opened her door and retrieved the sack of horns. As she turned back to the rail, she glanced at the Nissan and saw the front door opening.

Jonathan had seen it too. 'Now Gudrun! Now!'

She heard the alarm in his voice. Without a backward glance, she hurled the sack as far as she could throw it. Martin ducked, but it sailed over Ginny's head and splashed far out into the water.

Behind them, the Nissan's door slammed shut.

Gudrun had not known whether the horns would sink or not, because they were much lighter than they looked, so she had added a rock to the sack. After a moment's hesitation on the surface it vanished, leaving a few brief bubbles to mark what she considered to be a grave. They stood at the rail watching the spot until it was far behind them. A chapter had closed with the horns returning to a natural environment.

Watching the other ferry go past in the opposite direction with a similar load, Gudrun gripped Jonathan's arm and drew his attention to the queue they had left behind. It now contained a black Land Cruiser. 'He's not letting go. It's time we did something about it and take the fight to him.'

'You know what I think?' Jonathan was packing his passport away after they had cleared the Zambian immigration process – a minor bureaucratic headache which was more simple than he had anticipated. The much greater problem of what to do about the horns had been easily solved, staving off the threat of arrest – or worse, in Poh's hands. Combined, they had shoved his troubled imagination further back in his mind. 'I think we deserve a good lunch and a lazy afternoon.'

'Your planning, as usual, is excellent.' Ginny's face lit up in anticipation.

'Let's go straight to the hotel, have a drink and a bite there. Then we can walk it off by going to see the Eastern Cataract. It's not far, about a kilometre. We can check in to the campsite for the night later on.'

'Good plan.' Gudrun jumped into the front seat. 'What are we waiting for?'

My mood lightens, and immediately she's happier. She doesn't understand or simply doesn't see the problem I have with her. Perhaps I'm living in a different world. Is it me that isn't normal?

The hotel's lawn formed a gentle slope down to the riverbank. Several trees were dotted around, giving it a park-like feel with plenty of shade. A pleasant surprise for tourists was a herd of three semi-domesticated zebra grazing, at home with the nearby passage of humans. At the water's edge, an elevated deck provided an idyllic setting for eating, drinking or taking in the view.

Awed by the mighty river, all four were leaning over the balustrade and gazing downstream at the incredible volume of spray, which reached a height of twelve hundred feet or more when the river was in full flow. It was easy to understand why the Falls were called Mosi-oa-Tunya in the local language: *the smoke that thunders.*

The waiter brought their drinks and left some menus for them to study. Jonathan, Ginny and Martin left the railing and pulled up some chairs. Gudrun, in her floppy bush hat and sunglasses, stopped leaning over and turned to sit on the rail itself, hooked her feet between the balusters and faced the others. Most of her attention was directed to her right at the view, however. '*Sæti*, please ...' She held out a hand.

Jonathan rose to his feet, stretched and, without a change of expression, handed her her beer. She smiled her thanks and went back to studying the river.

'There's something unbeatable about the first one of the day.' Martin smacked his lips in appreciation and stroked the condensation off his glass. 'It's so refreshing.'

'And the second,' said Gudrun without turning her head.

Jonathan watched her. *How lucky I could be. Such a beautiful woman, and one with the same tastes as me. She's been so easy to get along with and so willing to get her hands dirty when the need arises. And her determination? It's misdirected at times, crazy, but I have to admire it. Being with her should be the ultimate in life, all I could ever want. I have to find a solution, and accept her as she is.*

She must have sensed something, because she turned, took off her sunglasses, met his eye and gave him a loving look.

If she's not worried about us, why should I be? Still, she knows there's something wrong, it's why she wants to talk. Why is it so difficult for me to span this gap I alone have created? If I can find a way, she'll have to meet me on the bridge, otherwise how can I be as affectionate as before? I want us to be okay, but all she's doing is putting distance between us.

Gudrun broke off the contact and looked towards the hotel. At once her mouth set into a thin line, and her stare intensified.

'Don't turn round, anyone,' she said. 'Poh is standing on the lawn staring down at us.' She dropped her gaze back to Jonathan. Her expression said it all: *I've had enough of this man.*

'He's gone into the trees. No. He's there again, higher up. He's joined two Asian men. Those big gym addicts are hovering nearby as well.'

With Poh's appearance, Jonathan was reminded of the threat still lurking in the background, an ugly scratch too deep to be polished out of the gleaming silver of their trip. Despite their apparent cheerfulness, the tension was rising amongst his friends.

Food and more drinks arrived. It always surprised Jonathan how much food Martin could eat. For such a small man, he put away enough for a horse, or, considering where they were, a zebra. He was the last to finish. 'Done,' he claimed with a satisfied hiccup. 'I'm now ready for a little nap before topping up tonight.'

'You'd better walk that off, little man, or you'll end up a small round ball of a creature,' Gudrun teased.

'I'm just trying to be big and strong like you.'

'Come on, let's go. We've done enough sitting in the past week, we need to move,' Jonathan said as he settled the bill.

He led them along the path to the Falls. It ran parallel to the river, through trees and bushes, before terminating at a point at the head of the Eastern Cataract. The river rushed past, the water white and turbulent a mere foot from the bank. Squatting, a person could put their hands in the water. Fall forward and, unless you were quick in grabbing a rock or tree root, the mighty current would take you, bounce you between rocks down a short slope, before carrying you into an almost free fall of over three hundred feet – not survivable. The odd contrast between the violence of the water and its harbouring of certain death, with the beauty of the rainbow in the spray, was both exciting and mesmerising, and their attention was gripped by a scene which would only release its hold with reluctance.

They were all standing less than a metre from the water. Martin was leaning on a sapling; Ginny, beside him, held his hand in both of hers as if to keep him safe. Jonathan was standing on a rock which protruded into the turbulence, with Gudrun behind, her arms wrapped round him and her chin resting on his shoulder. He was uncomfortable with the closeness of the contact in his current mood, but did not want to hurt her by moving away. However, something made him turn, and his head bumped hers. She stepped back out of his way with an annoyed, 'Ow!'

Behind them, not six feet away, stood Poh's two bodyguards, the same two who had been in the Johannesburg hotel. Both wore black T-shirts which emphasised their physique. Even the slightest movement caused a huge bicep to bulge and a pectoral muscle to twitch. Their expressions were unreadable, but their intentions were obvious. Retreat was not an option. There was no space to dodge, no strength to match what they possessed. Even the combined weight of all four friends would not be enough to win a scrum against these two.

Jonathan's voice was urgent but low. 'Martin!'

'What? Oh shit!'

One of the men flashed them a broad grin. 'Hello. Would you like a guide? We can show you around here. We know the guiding. You need your money changed? We know where to get the best rates. We know the Zim side as well, we can get you day pass to go there without a queue.'

Jonathan swallowed uncomfortably. This was back-to-the-wall stuff, if ever there was, except the wall was wet and final. Why was the man talking like this? The threat was obvious, so why offer them a way out? Or was he playing with them before they were pushed? He seemed to enjoy having the white tourists under his thumb. The other man's grim expression had not changed; he had not moved but for his eyes which flicked from one European to another. His upper body was huge; his arms would not hang at his sides.

Did Poh want them back at the hotel and this was not his killing ground after all? Was that what this was about? Come with us or we'll put you in the river?

'What do you want?' Gudrun's tone was aggressive.

'Cool it,' Jonathan hissed at her.

'We only want you to have the best time in our beautiful country, and we can show you around. Come with us, it will be worth it.'

Ginny made to move forward. The silent man stepped sideways, a casual move, but it blocked her.

There were only two ways out of this: believe him when he

said he would guide them, which might negate the immediate danger, or charge at them and hope to get through, which was a long shot. The man knew their options as well and his fixed smile showed he was enjoying their dilemma, maybe even looking forward to a struggle with a certain result?

Voices came from behind the men – a woman giggled, a man laughed. The bomb had been defused. Jonathan stepped forward and made room for the newcomers to get close to the water. Gudrun, Ginny and Martin followed suit. They stood with the other tourists, waited for them to return and walked with them as part of their group back towards the hotel.

The thugs let them go, but a shout of 'You don't want help?' carried all the menace of the previous few minutes, followed as it was with humourless laughter.

26

The campsite was not only that – there were also a few small rondavels available for greater comfort. Ginny and Martin had no tent and no bedding – it was still on their vehicle, miles down Hunter's Road – so were forced to take one of the small round huts.

They were assembled in the reception area. Jonathan turned to Gudrun. 'I think we should also take a rondavel for tonight. Poh and his bodybuilders made an obvious threat today, and there was the episode on Hunter's Road, which could have been the end of us. We'll sleep a lot easier behind a solid wall than under canvas.'

'Okay, but I'm seriously pissed off with this man.' Gudrun moved away from the desk, out of earshot of the receptionist. 'He's chasing us, he has us on the run, at a disadvantage. I don't like being in this position. Let's go on the attack and see how surprised he is and what he does.'

'You're right. I'm with you in principle, but we need to think what we can do since we're unarmed and are not cold-blooded killers. As you pointed out yourself, him being such a person gives him a huge advantage. But Gudrun, we are leaving these two out of it. This is not their fight and I won't have them put in danger.'

Ginny and Martin had finished check-in and joined them. 'Are you trying to send us home? Because if so, you can go and take a swim in the river.'

'No, but we were about to consider what we can do about Poh without involving you two.'

Ginny, surprisingly, took the lead from Martin. 'We're in about as much trouble as you are. If Poh goes for you, he has to kill us as well, because we'll be witnesses. Therefore we're sticking together, whether you like it or not. In any case, four is stronger than two.'

'Yeah,' said Martin, 'especially if you think of the size of those BBs.'

'BBs?'

'Sorry – Big Bruisers.'

The receptionist, who was working alone, came round the desk. 'Sahs, medems, I show you your huts.' He led them past a short line of light-green-painted rondavels to two at the end and pointed. 'These are yours. The bathroom for everybody is there, and you can park your car outside the hut, here.' He handed the keys to Martin and Jonathan. 'Extra-special guest coming tonight.' The man's face broke into a broad smile. 'Mister Heepo is coming.'

'Who?'

The receptionist, having had the same reaction from so many tourists, giggled. 'Mister Heepo, sah. He comes from the water in the night to eat here. I want you to be careful if you go out of your hut in the night. He knows humans, and he is not dangerous if you leave him alone. But please, do not go close to him. Look around the corner before you go around the corner. You can go the other side of a hut to miss him. He will know you there, but he won't be angry unless you catch him by surprise. You can take a photo, he won't be angry, but don't go close, please.'

'Wow! That's exciting. It makes a change from Poh. Poh and Hee-Poh.' Martin laughed through his handkerchief, which had not been returned to his pocket since they had arrived there. 'The bloody pollen they have here is getting to me.'

Grouped at the Land Rover with beers in hand, they continued to discuss what they should do about Poh. It was an inexhaustible subject. Jonathan summed up all their ideas. 'Whatever action we take has to be either long-lasting or final. We have to get the man out of our hair until Webb is ready to have him arrested. Anything less is a waste of time and carries the risk of being arrested ourselves. Even if he did get the first pair of horns off Rider, he wouldn't carry such incriminating evidence around with him, although he's sure to have lots of cash. So breaking into his hotel room would be high risk with doubtful reward, and it won't stop him trying to kill us. Besides, we already have photographic proof of a transaction, plus my sighting of him in Mozambique.'

Nods of agreement.

Jonathan went on, 'I don't see how getting him arrested on some trumped-up charge like assault – thanks for volunteering, Gudrun – is going to help, because he'll just buy his way out of it. If we lured him back into South Africa, we can't be certain Webb is ready to arrest him, so it might take too long with him still hunting us.

'We have to stop him. Finality is necessary, which means he either has to be killed or put in hospital for a while. I am not prepared to kill him, and I don't like the idea of deliberate injury, even with a person like him. Besides, his BBs will still be around.'

'I will do it,' Gudrun's lip curled to show her teeth. 'I could kill an evil man to save another human, and I could kill an evil man to save animals. I'd put this bastard in hospital without any qualms whatsoever.'

Jonathan tapped his fingers on the bonnet. 'Gudrun, this is not a James Bond movie. This is real life. You do not have it in you to kill anyone, even Poh. You're angry now, but when you get to the point of pulling the trigger or sticking the knife in, you wouldn't do it. Yes, you would injure him, I'm sure you would, but remember his bodyguards will still do what he tells them from his hospital bed. And,' he emphasised, 'you won't want to spend years in an African prison.'

He was becoming used to her signs of frustration when she knew he was right.

Ginny broke the difficult silence that followed. 'We're all exhausted, and we're not thinking rationally. I propose we sleep on these ideas without taking any action. It's a risk, but we're not in a position to do much else. We've no weapons, and it would be useless going to the police for protection, so we should be vigilant tonight, somehow, and get some sleep.'

'We could simply drive away somewhere,' said Martin.

'I'm sick of running away from this man, I want to face him,' said Gudrun, her tone sharp.

Jonathan shook his head. Would it be possible for him to keep this woman in check for the rest of his life?

Martin, the man for whom food and drink were of paramount importance, defused the tension. 'Time to get a barbecue going and eat something. Who wants another beer?'

As the last vestige of light left the sky, Jonathan put another few pieces of wood on the fire. The flames stretched up to the lower branches of an acacia before settling. Later, sated with their meal, the four of them sat in silence, sipping their drinks and staring into the blaze. No one added any more fuel, and the fire soon subsided into a mass of glowing coals.

'I'm for bed,' Gudrun announced. 'I feel exhausted tonight.'

'Me too,' said Ginny.

Jonathan doused the remnants of the fire with water. 'I think we're all in need of sleep. Make sure your door's locked, Martin, this afternoon's encounter with Poh's men has put me a bit on edge.'

'And mind Mister Heepo if you go to the loo,' said Martin, laughing.

'Sit down Jonathan. We need to talk.' Gudrun pointed to one of the beds. She didn't follow suit, but strode around the limited space in the rondavel for a minute while he put himself through agony in anticipation of what she was about to say.

'What is the matter with you? You've withdrawn into yourself, you don't treat me like you used to. We have argued a few times, but so what? Everybody argues. Are you going off me? Do you want to end our relationship? I need to know what's wrong so we can fix it.'

Jonathan didn't answer, just stared down at his hands. This was it, the moment he had been dreading. The critical, terrible discussion about their future which could end in disaster, ripping every fibre of feeling from him, leaving him as sad, floppy and useless as a deflated balloon.

'Well?'

'This can't go on, you know.'

'What?'

'You cannot continue to disregard the effects your actions will have on other people.'

'Are you still on about that?'

'Gudrun, can't you see how this affects our relationship? You cannot separate your actions in fighting Poh from how it affects us. You put other people in danger to achieve what you want, and it doesn't seem to worry you. That is not how I play the game, and it's creating a serious difference between us.'

She stopped her pacing and sat on her bed, facing him. 'Jonathan, all couples have different opinions on things, but they don't let them get in the way of a sound relationship. You need to learn to separate issues and tackle each one on its own. We just have different points of view on this. Get over it, accept it. What we're arguing about is not a problem for me. It doesn't affect what I feel for you.'

With the discussion he had been dreading now well under way, Jonathan's confidence rose. 'We're not talking about minor issues here. We're talking about people's lives being put at risk. I find your attitude extremely hard to deal with, and I would love to find a solution. If I could change, I would, but I don't think it's up to me. You need to make an effort with this, Gudrun, you've got to meet me half way.'

'Don't try to change me, Jonathan.'

'Why would I want to change what I love? Until a year ago, I was under constant pressure from my father and Lisa and her parents to do what they thought was best for me. In fact it was what was best for them, of course, so I rebelled and walked out. I know what it's like when someone tries to make you into something you're not, and I won't do it to you or anyone else. All I'm asking is for you to think what the repercussions of your actions will be before you go to war.'

Gudrun greeted his comment with a long silence. It was her turn to study her hands; she appeared to be struggling to say what she wanted to. She shook her head as if to rid it of previous thoughts. He saw a tear trickling down the left side of her nose. She gave it a rough swipe. 'I can't help it. When something important has to be done, I have to do it immediately, and I cannot rest until it's complete. I suppose it's a need for success, but I won't allow anything to stand in my way. I know I'm wrong sometimes like you say, but I get consumed by this need for justice, for this barbaric activity to stop, for Poh and his cronies to be taken out. I must win – I *will* win.'

Speaking calmly as he sought to lessen the tension, he said, 'When you've taken out Poh, others will fill his place – they're already doing the same thing. All you're achieving is the postponement of a rhino's death. The poor animal will suffer the same fate at the hands of other bloody humans.'

'I know, but it'll be a battle won. And lots of victories will win the war.'

'Winning this war will involve a lot more than taking out the likes of Poh. The whole culture in the Far East has to change. Gudrun, I'm trying to put your efforts in perspective. What you're doing is right, and I'm with you all the way, but do you want to see our friends killed or injured in the process?'

'Of course not.'

'How do we solve this? How can we manage it so that when you feel impulsive you stop and think?'

She didn't answer, and in the silence which followed, Jonathan tried to assemble his thoughts. *Perhaps that's my role. I don't want to stop you doing what you want to do, and I don't believe I could. But maybe I can help channel your rage, your aggression and your demand for instant action into a direction where it can do less harm. But you must, you absolutely must, listen to what I say.*

He blurted out the one thing he never wanted to hear. 'If we cannot reach some agreement on how to live our lives, I don't see how we can continue. I love you, you know that, and the last thing I want is for us to break apart.' He put a hand over his mouth. *Why did I say that? How bloody stupid!*

Gudrun stood and took the single pace forward to reach him. She towered over him. 'Stand up,' she ordered.

He obeyed, but she put a hand out to his chest anyway, lifted him upright by his shirt and held him at arm's length.

Why is she so aggressive? Did I put my foot in it? Is she about to do something crazy?

'You are my life, Jonathan. Don't ever mention breaking up, or I'll come after you with a will you have never seen in me before.' She moved closer and held him so tight he could only take shallow breaths.

He laughed in relief and kissed her hard.

27

A black Land Cruiser crawled along the track leading to the campsite, crunching the dirt as it drifted to a stop. Its lights died. Poh, in the front passenger seat, peeled a number of notes from a wad he took from his hip pocket and handed them to the driver. Not a word was spoken. The muscle-bound African walked with that odd, legs-apart gait which is a product of over-developed thighs. With his black trousers and black T-shirt, he made a formidable outline striding towards the office lights.

An hour later, Poh checked his watch and indicated to the driver. They got out, pushed the car doors so they only gave a soft click, and walked towards the line of huts.

In front of them was the toilet block, behind it a path demarcated by logs along its sides and a few low-level lights to ensure guests did not stray into the bush in the night. Avoiding the lights of the path as long as possible, they passed round the back of the bathrooms. Poh was leading, the bodyguard towering behind the little man. Martin and Ginny's hut was in front of him, Jonathan and Gudrun's to the right.

Poh stopped. The bruiser was so close he bumped into him. An enormous bulbous shape loomed in front, silhouetted against the path lights and not two metres away. The sound of grass being torn from the ground was clear. Poh backed away, holding his breath. At the shoulder, the hippo was only a foot shorter than he was and weighed a good one and a half tons. To knock into one of the most dangerous beasts in Africa would be the end. Without taking his eyes off the animal, he signalled his muscleman to retreat. When they were clear, Poh looked back. The animal was still feeding, but beyond him there was a movement in the soft lights of the path.

The two of them reached the walkway at the other end of the bathrooms. Poh peered at his watch and looked around. From the river side of the camp, the unmistakable outline of his other bodyguard appeared. A short whispered conversation, and the three passed round the rear of Martin's hut.

Gudrun woke some time after midnight. It was hot in the rondavel, and she needed the bathroom. The hut was equipped with two single beds, each with its own mosquito net suspended from the open thatch, so getting up without disturbing a snoring Jonathan was easy. She pulled on her jeans and a shirt and went to the door, which was locked with a simple Yale night latch. She couldn't find the key in the dark, so she pushed up the snib to hold the latch open and went outside. It was much cooler in the night air, and she stood for a moment while she searched for Mister Heepo. Three steps along the path and she heard the sound of grass being ripped apart. She peered to the left, a little ahead of her, and could just make out his massive bulk. She could see nothing beyond the animal – it was too black in the bush on the far side of the lights. He – was it a he? – was too close to the walkway to pass without disturbing him, so Gudrun detoured to the right, putting Martin's hut between her and the creature. Past the hut and back on the path, Gudrun went into the toilet block.

When she came out, she peered around to see where the great beast was, and again heard the tearing of grass. He was still where she'd left him, so she took the same route back to her hut, to the rear of Martin's. *Jonathan must come and see this. He'll be thrilled.*

A rough hand was slapped over her mouth. Something hard and metallic was pressed against her neck. She struggled, but he was far too strong; she couldn't move. His breath stank, his fingers smelled of greasy food and he could not have washed in days. Her stomach churned and threatened to vomit. Poh came into her view. He glared up at her, his narrow eyes glinting in the dim light: black and hard as jet. He turned and led the way to her hut.

The door opened with a slight push. Jonathan was still snoring. Gudrun winced as a gun was rammed against his throat. He choked, struggling against the sheet and the mosquito net. The second bruiser ripped the net out of the roof and encased him in it; as trussed as a spider's fly. Poh's gun was always in full view and aimed at his face.

Jonathan opened his mouth to speak but snapped it shut as BB One pushed his gun into Gudrun's neck.

With Poh's pistol steady an inch from Jonathan's temple, BB Two released him by cutting the net away with a knife. Twice Jonathan's arms were slashed in the process. Blood dripped onto the sheet. Freed, he stood, dressed only in his underpants. Two grabbed Jonathan's clothes off the chair and tossed them at him. His mind racing, he took his time in getting dressed. But there was nothing he could do; there were three of them and even one of the BBs could deal with both him and Gudrun – and they had guns.

They were moved outside. Neither Poh nor his men spoke at all. Every move was dictated by gestures.

'Who did you buy,' Jonathan asked, 'Mueller or his assistant?'

Poh's voice was more oriental than African. 'Mueller not need money.'

'Did you buy the other horns from Rider?'

'Yes.'

'Where are you taking us?'

'For swim.'

Two laughed next to Jonathan's ear. It was a spittle-laden, ghee, ghee, sort of sound, high-pitched and eerie.

'Why haven't you tied us up? Why leave us free to fight you?'

'You no win fight. I no want evidence of tie-up on your body. You have accident when you found.'

'So you won't shoot us either then?'

'You try fight, we shoot. Better not shoot – no evidence. You fight, I shoot. Same end for you – in water.'

They continued in silence to the riverbank. As they walked, a break in the trees ahead let in a brilliant quarter moon. A ribbon of silver gave an almost undisturbed reflection off the steady water nearby, but further out it was broken and turbulent and told of rapids.

A boat was drawn up onto a muddy beach. It was long and narrow, had six seats on benches and a single outboard motor, which struck Jonathan as risky in such dangerous waters. *What would happen if the engine failed? The current to the Falls is not something you can swim against. That's what's planned for us.*

BB One shoved Gudrun towards the boat, and pushed her again to force her into it; Two followed with Jonathan. Poh stood watching, a couple of metres away. One raised his pistol to Gudrun's temple. She sat on the nearest seat. He took the one beside her.

BB Two left Jonathan unguarded and lifted the front of the boat, pushing it off the mud and into the water. It drifted sideways in the gentle current close to the shore. Poh held the mooring rope while Two boarded and turned his attention back to his captive. Poh waded calf-deep and pulled the bow around.

Jonathan looked at Gudrun. Her eyes were soft in the moonlight, holding him, caressing him. All their love was in her look. They knew their situation was helpless. Do something stupid and get shot, or do nothing and be dumped overboard to be taken over the Falls in the mighty current. His voice was low and hoarse. 'This may be the last time we see each other. I love you.'

'I know you do. Me too. At least we'll go together if we can't stop this.'

Gudrun broke her gaze and glanced around. Jonathan followed her eyes towards the moon's trace and joined her in absorbing its beauty for the last time. She stiffened as her attention was gripped by a movement on the water. A ripple on the surface was tracking steadily towards the boat. He knew what it was; she knew what it was. Fascinated, they stayed silent and waited.

The shallows erupted. The monster leapt, clearing the surface. With an audible snap, its jaws clamped on flesh. It splashed down into the mud and rolled, giving a flash of its off-white belly. Poh's hideous scream pierced the night. His body was flung in a high arc, crashing down onto the side of the boat. The crocodile's head itself smashed the gunwale and hit One a glancing blow. The boat tipped and threw them all into the water, right next to the thrashing croc.

One had dropped his gun. Two had not; he stood and took aim. Gudrun threw herself at him, both hands gripping his arm and ruining his shot. He ripped the gun free and turned it on her.

Jonathan hit him and hurt his own fist, but the man staggered off balance. The croc was retreating into the deeper water with Poh firm in its jaws. As it went, it threw the body from side to side ripping flesh from bone. It had no interest in any other prey, one victim was enough for now, but the body struck Two in the legs and knocked him flat. He recovered and scrambled from the river after One, who was already on the bank. They stood staring down at the two tourists for a moment, before walking away without a word.

Jonathan took Gudrun's hand and hurried her up the bank. 'There might be another one out there.'

Safe above the water, they sat side by side. She rested her head on his shoulder. In silence they stared at the moon and its reflection while their nerves settled.

'Bloody hell. Saved by the devil,' Jonathan said softly.

'No, Poh was the devil. A croc is a croc.'

'You're right. You were also right not to warn him – I was about to shout when it struck.'

'That's because you're a good man. I wanted revenge for that poor rhino. Poh deserved to die. I will have no regrets.' She took both his arms and pushed his sleeves up his forearms for him. 'There.' She smiled, stood and extended a hand to him. 'I must shower. That man hadn't washed in a week, and his stench is sticking to my clothes.'

'I think we should let the others sleep. We can tell them all about this later.'

'Yes. After my shower …'

'And mine …'

'I want to share a single bed until we get up.'

'We've still got an hour before boarding. Let's get a beer, Martin; the girls can indulge in some retail therapy in the duty-free.'

Martin made slurping noises. 'Brilliant idea.'

Gudrun made a face at him and grinned at Ginny, but Jonathan gripped her arm and pointed. 'There's Rider – at the door of the First Class lounge.'

'Bastard!'

'I'll call Webb, he gave me his private number.' Jonathan had already switched his phone off. It took forever to crawl back into life. He searched for Rider, but he had disappeared.

'Mike, sorry to call you so late. We've just seen Mickey Rider. He must be on our flight. I don't know what strings you can pull, but there's still over twelve hours before we arrive at Heathrow.'

The others studied his face as the conversation ended.

'What's going on?'

'Ginny, Poh admitted to me that he had bought the first horns from Rider. Webb, and whatever police help he has, had lost track of Mickey so they could do nothing about it. I don't know what Mike Webb can do now, but he's got a lot of contacts and influence.'

'But you said Rider didn't see Poh in the village, so how did he know to approach him?'

'Well, I thought – assumed – he'd already gone into the bush, but I must have been wrong.'

'Cheers.' Martin raised his glass. 'Here's to a good flight. The aircraft's not full, so we might be able to spread out a bit.'

'It's all right for you two miniature people, but Gudrun and I are in for an uncomfortable night. Love, we have to start earning enough money to travel in First Class like Rider, but at least we're near the front of Economy, so we can get off ahead of the greater mass.'

'At the moment wealth is about as fat a chance as winning the lottery.'

'Tell me, Jonathan,' said Ginny, 'with all the drama of this trip, your experience in Mozambique, what we've been through being hunted by Poh and your narrow escape on the river the other night, are you still happy with the choice you made? Or would you rather be safe at home with Lisa?'

He laughed. 'That's a no-brainer. Every choice we humans make has consequences. In choosing to live this life instead of the alternative of a conventional marriage, kids and a business, I've been bloody uncomfortable, and Barry Castle and his psychopathic twins almost killed me – us. Poh almost killed us. It doesn't matter, I love what's happened. It's such a great feeling to go through it all and survive. It's been stimulating and inspirational, which, as you know, is what I live for. The greatest reward, though, was finding Gudrun.'

That earned him a crushing hug and a long kiss.

On board, Ginny and Martin settled into the row behind them. Jonathan was putting his things into the overhead bin when he looked sideways to see a cabin attendant putting an old lady's bag up for her.

'Claire!'

'Jonathan, Gudrun! How wonderful, welcome on board.' She was smart and pretty in her uniform. She gave them both a tight hug. 'How fantastic. I can't chat now, but later I want to hear all about your trip. God, was that ever an experience?' She darted away to help other passengers.

Before the doors closed, Claire came back. 'I've got you an upgrade to Premium Economy. I can't get you in Business, it's full, but there are two adjacent seats in Premium. You can move after take-off.'

'That's kind, Claire, but our friends are here.' Jonathan indicated behind him.

Martin waved him a dismissal. 'Don't be stupid *all* your life, Jonathan, take the offer. We've seen enough of you two for a while anyway!'

With dinner behind them and the cabin lights switched off, Jonathan led Gudrun into the galley. Claire had her mouth open much of the time as Gudrun gave a brief run-down of what had happened after they left the Kruger Park.

'You two certainly know how to attract trouble. When I decided on that trip, I had just broken up with my fiancé. It was intended to be a sort of therapy. I suppose it was, actually, because the experience taught me a lot about life, how valuable it is. Anyway, thanks to my forced change of outlook, James and I made up. We're getting married in a couple of months. I'm over the moon!' She dabbed at her eyes. 'Out of everything bad comes something good, don't you think?'

'We had to cut our plans short because of the horn theft and Poh's death,' said Jonathan, and teased, 'We still have to complete the second half of the trip through Botswana and Namibia. You, your fiancé and Kathy can come for free.'

'Ha, bloody ha. I think we'll both be working then – in fact I'm sure we are. I've had as much scary stuff as I can take in one year, thank you.'

Gudrun put a hand on Claire's arm. 'We should get together.'

'Of course we must. I'll drag that wicked Kathy over too. She's on a Hong Kong flight at the moment.'

'What happened to Annette? I felt so bad about her, and you two did such a wonderful job looking after her.'

'The French Embassy took over everything, but we managed to contact her sister in France and saw her off on her flight home, poor thing. She was broken by Armand's death, by the way he died – it was so unnecessary. All for the want of an EpiPen. And the fact she had to leave him there destroyed her. I spoke to her sister again later. She said the French authorities are trying to recover his body.'

'And Hudson?' said Gudrun.

'Hudson was super. He went his own way at the end, but he made a special effort to come and say goodbye before we left. We never saw Rider again. I can't say that worried me.'

'I hate to be the bearer of bad news,' Jonathan said, 'but Mickey is in First Class.'

After twenty minutes in the holding pattern above Heathrow, the taxi from the runway took forever. The seat belt signs went out at last, and the usual rush to be off the aircraft began. Claire and some other cabin crew manned the doors. First and Business Class passengers shuffled towards the exit ahead of the Economy crowd, where Jonathan stood at the front of his queue, Gudrun behind him. Both were watching with interest.

Mickey Rider appeared behind a slow-moving old lady, impatience radiating from him. His eyes lifted to see Jonathan. Almost imperceptible surprise flickered across his face before he looked away.

Claire and another team member stood in the cabin

doorway, thanking and wishing the departing guests well. When Rider passed, her polite smile turned sour.

They were released.

'I'll call you – soon,' Claire said to Gudrun as they passed through into the tunnel.

Rider was near the front of the queue for the electronic passport gates, Jonathan and Gudrun some twenty people behind him. Rider stood in front of the camera. It was taking a long time to recognise him. He shifted about, but the light would not change from red to green and the doors would not open. Irritated and muttering, he left the gate and passed round the side to the immigration officer in the booth.

The official was asking Rider questions without returning his passport. Two other Border Force officers stepped forward. Rider looked back as they came to stand one on either side of him.

Jonathan grinned at Mickey and gave him a contemptuous wave.

* * *

Before You Go

Thank you for reading *Nature's Justice*. If you enjoyed the book and have a moment to spare, writing a short review on Amazon, Goodreads or your favourite site would be greatly appreciated. Authors depend on reader opinions in order to produce enjoyable works. Reviews help authors to further their careers.

Please feel free to pick up the next sequel, *The Pilot*, to find out how Jonathan's alter ego, Cuff, copes with the life he has chosen.

To find out more about the author and his works please visit:
https://www.helifish.co.uk where you have the option to subscribe to his mailing list.

You can also find him on Facebook: http://www.facebook.com/casole75
and on Twitter: @helifish74

I look forward to hearing from you.

Also by CA Sole

The Scott Series:

In ***Scott's Choice*** Cuthbert Jonathan Scott is a young man with a dominant adventurous spirit. He grew up being indoctrinated by his father into an approach to life that was completely at odds with his nature: take no risks, caution in everything, settle down while young, save your money, on and on. A random event results in a decisive moment. He is torn between two options: following his father's teaching or being himself.

Two personae emerge. One, Jonathan, begins a life following his natural instincts. His spirit of adventure predominates. His choice has consequences which bring several life-threatening events but also great rewards.

Jonathan's alter ego, Cuff, is the brainwashed youth who tries to adopt the more cautious approach. But his nature conflicts with this and leads him on a dangerous path to escape the mundane existence which was the consequence of his choice. It seems he cannot avoid risk. Indeed, danger appears to seek him out.

Two independent stories develop in ***Scott's Choice***. The tales are linked only by his friends and enemies who continue to influence and react to events in Cuff's life in one way, and in Jonathan's life in another. However, certain events are common to both and fixed in the calendar.

***

The Pilot is the second sequel to ***Scott's Choice***. Cuff Scott tries to follow a career to become an airline pilot, but his attempts to lead a stable and prosperous life are ruined by events.

At the flying school where he instructs, he becomes aware of someone smuggling illegal immigrants into the country by night. That's not his only problem. His student is being stalked by an increasingly dangerous man, and she thinks it's him.

It seems that trouble seeks him out and brings his inherent instinct for adventure to the fore. He is forced to question if he's really the persona he's trying to be.

#

A Fitting Revenge is a thriller about extraordinary events that happen to ordinary people.

Your friends are in deep trouble. What if you take a step too far in avenging them?

In southern rural England, Alastair is helping his close friend to avoid a punishing divorce from Sandra. But Sandra is ruthless, merciless and determined to win.

As Alastair is drawn into a situation which he battles to control, the love binding him and Juliet is ripped apart.

With the common goal of rescuing their friend, they strive to work together, but the tension between them only widens the rift as Alastair faces the ruination of his life.

Fighting his way out of the turmoil, Alastair stretches reason to exact a terrible revenge for the extortion and assault that has affected his friends. In doing so, he discovers a side to himself which he never knew existed.

Revenge must be taken, but is Alastair's 'eye for an eye' concept too extreme? Will Juliet remain a love lost?

The Author

CA Sole began writing in 1990 with a thriller titled Zahak's Breath. An agent took it on and, after a few not insignificant changes, submitted it to a publisher. The first rejection dented his ego and left its mark! Colin took the extraordinary and foolish step of giving up his full-time job to write in 1995. His confidence took another hit, and he had to return to work for enough money to buy beer. He persevered, wrote a couple of short stories and about half a novel. That short manuscript has been incorporated into one of the sequels of the Scott series.

Colin's first published novel, *A Fitting Revenge*, came out in 2016 and quickly received 4- and 5-star reviews on Amazon and Goodreads. His second book, CJ, was done through a small publisher and also received a small number of 4- and 5-star reviews. However, Colin's lack of enthusiasm (and plain laziness) over marketing resulted in poor sales. CJ has been rewritten and published in the summer of 2019 as *Scott's Choice*. It has two sequels: *Nature's Justice* and *The Pilot*.

Having been in the British Army, a professional helicopter pilot and an aviation consultant, his work has taken him all over the world to some 66 countries. He lived and worked in Africa – North, South, East and West – for 43 years before returning to England for good. It's therefore not surprising that the background to Colin's books is travel.

* * *

There is far too much of the less trodden world left to see.

To find out more about CA Sole's works and future projects, please visit: https://www.helifish.co.uk